Death Paints a Picture

Black Curtain Press
PO Box 632
Floyd VA 24091

ISBN 13: 978-1627550789

First Edition
10 9 8 7 6 5 4 3 2 1

Death Paints a Picture

Miles Burton

Chapter I

At three o'clock in the afternoon of Wednesday, 14th June, Mr. Paul Clapdale left his house on the borders of the fishing village of Port Bosun. He had had his lunch and a siesta, and was now ready for a chat with his friend George Hawken.

Mr. Clapdale was in the early seventies, short and tubby. His eyes were bright blue, and his hair and closely trimmed beard iron grey. In summer he habitually wore a grey suit, except on Sundays, when he dressed in blue. When he went out, he carried a heavy stick, not so much as a means of support, but to brandish as he walked. He had by now become a familiar figure in Port Bosun, where he had lived for the past seven years.

He had come to live there on his retirement at the age of sixty-five. Until then, he had managed the not inconsiderable business which he owned in Yorkshire. He was a widower, with a married son and a married daughter. He did not now see very much of either of them. The son had taken over the management of the business, which only left him sufficient leisure to visit his father at long intervals. The daughter lived with her husband, who was a surveyor in Edinburgh.

But Mr. Clapdale did not live alone. He had as his companion his devoted sister Janet, ten years younger than himself. Brother and sister were almost exactly alike, but for the fact that Janet did not wear a beard.

In spite of the disadvantage of not being natives, and therefore to be regarded with suspicion, both Paul and Janet had become popular in Port Bosun. It should be remarked that the name of the village had nothing to do with boatswains. It was a corruption of the old Cornish word "Bosant," meaning holy.

Very soon after he had settled in Port Bosun, Paul had made the acquaintance of George Hawken, a man a couple of years older than himself. George, who had never married, had devoted the greater part of his life to painting. His work had never been favourably received, perhaps because it was too imaginative. Now and then he had sold a picture, and this sufficed for his modest requirements. He lived by himself and employed no helper. He did all the housework, and took a pride in doing it efficiently. He was wont to say that there could be as much art in cooking and washing up as in painting pictures.

Paul's route took him downhill to the centre of the village, which lay clustered round the tiny harbour. He rounded the head of this, and then ascended again, leaving the village behind him. He followed the road, hardly more than a lane, for about a quarter of a mile. This brought him to George's cottage. It had originally consisted of four rooms, two on the ground floor and two above but, many years before, George had had a studio added to it.

A short path led from the road to the cottage. Paul walked along this and hammered on the door. He got no reply, but this did not surprise him, George was more than slightly deaf, and if he was working in the studio he might not have heard the knock. He opened the door without ceremony and walked in.

The door opened into the kitchen, which was scrupulously tidy. From this another door opened into the front room. Paul passed through and crossed the room to another door, which was shut. He opened it and entered the studio, hung with a quantity of George's unsold pictures. Queer things they were, Paul had always thought. Rocks and stones and sand, always with the sea in the background. Nothing, in Paul's opinion, of any interest. He couldn't imagine anyone wanting to live with any of them.

However, the studio, so familiar to him, was empty. George must have gone out, to sketch, no doubt. Paul had an idea where to look for him. He left the cottage and returned to the road, which he followed for a couple of hundred yards to a spot where a footpath branched off from it.

The road continued along the top of the cliffs, overlooking the sea. But the path dipped slightly, until it reached a ledge running along the face of the cliff, about half-way up. The ledge was of varying width, mainly narrow but broadening out here and there into comparatively wide stretches. It did not run straight, since it followed the irregularities of the cliff face. At no point was it possible to see more than a few yards along it. It was bounded on one side by the almost vertical wall of the upper cliff, and on the other by the sea.

Paul knew that the ledge was George's favourite ground from which to sketch. He walked along it, expecting to come upon George at any moment. But he had gone some little distance before he came upon any sign of him. Then, as he turned a corner of the rock, he came out into one of the wider spaces. There, lying on the ground, was the shooting-stick on which George always sat when he was making sketches, and beside it a sketching block and a pencil. But of George there was nothing to be seen.

Paul was very much astonished. George would never have hurried away, leaving his belongings in such disorder. Paul called out his name which echoed and reechoed from the surrounding rocks. But there was no reply. Paul felt a sudden sense of misgiving. He walked to the seaward edge of the ledge and looked over.

It was a still afternoon, with no wind. The sea was perfectly smooth, and had that glassy look which sometimes results from a flat calm. At the foot of the cliffs was a stretch of comparatively level rock, upon which the little wavelets of the flowing tide were beginning to encroach. And on this level surface, immediately below the spot on which Paul stood, lay an inert figure. The corduroy trousers and alpaca jacket, so familiar to Paul, told him that it was George.

He wasted no time, but hurried back by the way he had come. Along the ledge to the road and down it to the village. The constable's house was close beside the harbour, and Paul made his way to it. He found Constable Docking at home, and told him his story.

"How Mr. Hawken came to fall over the cliff I can't imagine,," he went on. "And what's to be done? If he wasn't already dead when I saw him, he must be drowned by now, as the tide is rising."

"We must recover the body," Docking replied. "And from what you tell me, Mr. Clapdale, it seems that the best way to do that will be by boat. We shall have to get a fisherman to help us there. The Penwarnes have got a small boat. They must be ashore, because their bigger boat, the Seabird, is in the harbour. If you'll wait here, I'll go and find them."

Docking went off. The Penwarnes lived only a hundred

yards away, and he found three of the four brothers at home. They were a dour, rugged family, who earned their living by fishing. Docking repeated to them Paul's story.

"He's got to be picked up," he said. "I'm wondering if you could take me round in your small boat?"

"Yes, we'll do that," Jake, the eldest of the three replied. "Mr. Hawken, you say? That's bad. We've always looked on him as one of us. Amos and I will get the boat alongside the steps. You'd better ask Mr. Clapdale to go and stand at the place he saw Mr. Hawken from then we shall know which way to steer."

Docking went back to his house, and told Paul what he wanted him to do. Paul set off at once, and very soon reached the spot. Looking over the cliff, he saw that the tide had risen sufficiently to cover the body which was still visible under the water. It was rolling slowly from side to side under the influence of the current.

Paul had not long to wait before the boat came out of the harbour entrance. The two Penwarne brothers were rowing, and Docking sat in the stern. Seeing Paul standing on the ledge, they steered towards him. As they neared the foot of the cliff, Jake laid down his oar and stood in the bows of the boat, looking downwards. There was by now sufficient water to float the boat over the flat rocks. Paul pointed to where he could see the body, and Jake raised his hand in acknowledgment.

It was not very long before he and his brother had lifted it into the boat.

They rowed back to the harbour and brought the boat alongside the steps. Docking went to his house and rang up Dr. Godney, who lived in the village. He found him at home, and told him what had happened.

"I'm going to get Mr. Hawken's body to his cottage, Doctor," he said. "Could you come along there and see it?"

Godney promised to do this and Docking returned to the steps, taking a wheeled-stretcher with him. He and the Penwarne brothers lifted the body from the boat and laid it on the stretcher. Then, with the assistance of Amos, Docking wheeled it up the road towards the cottage.

Before they reached it, they met Paul coming towards them.

"You'd better come with us, Mr. Clapdale," said Docking. "I've never been inside Mr. Hawken's cottage, so I don't know my way about. Where had we best put the body? The doctor is coming along to see it."

"I suggest the kitchen table," Paul replied. "It's the most convenient place. The doctor will be able to examine it there."

The stretcher was wheeled up to the cottage door. Paul opened it, and between them they lifted the body on to the kitchen table. Amos offered to take the stretcher back to Docking's house and went off with it. Paul and Docking remained in the kitchen, where George's sodden clothing dripped steadily on to the floor.

They had not been waiting very long when Dr. Godney's car drew up outside the gate. Docking went out to meet the doctor.

"The body's in the kitchen here, Doctor," he said. "I'll show you the way."

Godney alighted from the car, carrying his bag, and following Docking into the kitchen.

"Good afternoon, Clapdale," he said. "Docking tells me that it was you who saw Mr. Hawken lying at the foot of the cliff?"

"That's right," Paul replied. "I can't imagine how it happened. George knew every inch of that ledge in the face of the cliff. He was always sketching from it."

"He could hardly have survived a fall from that height," said Godney. "Help me to take his clothes off, Constable."

When the clothes had been removed, Godney carried out a thorough external examination.

"He didn't die of drowning," he said at last. "As one might have expected, he was dead before the water rose and covered him. The injuries he received from his fall must have been immediately fatal. A fractured skull and a broken neck, to say nothing of minor injuries. And there's another thing I don't understand. A red mark completely encircling the neck. It may be a natural blemish. You knew him well, I believe, Clapdale. Had you ever noticed it?"

"I can't say that I had," Paul replied. "In summer, George was nearly always dressed as he was to-day. An open shirt with no collar. If the mark had been there, I am certain that I should have noticed it."

"Well, the coroner is sure to ask the pathologist to examine the body," said Godney. "Perhaps he'll be able to offer an explanation. Mr. Hawken must have fallen from the cliff some time before you saw him, Clapdale. My opinion is that he died some eight hours ago."

"It's a quarter to five now," said Docking. "That means that he fell from the cliff about nine o'clock this morning."

"George was often out as early as that," Paul remarked. "He'd go sketching at any time he thought the light was right."

"Well, there it is," said Godney. "For the sake of decency, we ought to find something with which to cover the body."

"I can do that," Paul replied. He left the kitchen and went upstairs to George's bedroom, where he took a sheet from the bed. This he took downstairs and spread it over the body. Godney, having undertaken to inform the coroner, returned to his car and drove away.

"There's no more we can do here," said Docking. "I'm sorry to have to trouble you, Mr. Clapdale. But would you be good enough to show me the place from which you saw Mr. Hawken?"

"By all means," Paul replied. "It's no trouble. If you'll come with me, I'll gladly show you."

"Thank you, Mr. Clapdale," said Docking. "But we shall have to lock up this house first."

The key of the outer door was in the lock on the inside. Docking took it out, and he and Paul passed out. He locked the door behind them and put the key in his pocket.

"It was soon after three when I looked in to see if George was at home," said Paul as they set off. "When I found that he wasn't, I guessed where he might be. For the last few weeks he had been sketching from the ledge. That was the way he always worked. He would make a series of sketches then, using them as a guide, would paint a picture in the studio. I went to look for him, and found his shooting-stick and sketching block. You'll see for yourself in a few minutes. I left them where they were."

"Do you know if Mr. Hawken had any relations?" Docking asked.

"Yes, I can tell you about them," Paul replied. "His elder brother Sir Matthew Hawken is alive. He was, in his time, quite a famous painter, and made a lot of money, so they say. He went in for portraits mainly and painted a number of distinguished people. George told me that his brother was knighted as a reward for painting a member of the Royal Family. You know, I dare say, that the Hawkens are natives of Port

Bosun?"

"Yes, I've heard that," said Docking. "And I've been told that Mr. George Hawken's father was a fisherman."

"That's correct," Paul replied. "George himself told me that. He was not ashamed of his humble origins. It's curious that both the sons should have taken to painting. But to return to Sir Matthew. It would be no good getting in touch with him, because he's an invalid, and can't get about. He lives at a place called Moat Barn. I don't know the precise address, but it's somewhere in the south of England. But George had two nephews, the sons of his sister, now dead."

"Do you know where they are to be found?" Docking asked.

"I can tell you something about the elder nephew, Hubert Benson," Paul replied. "He is married, and is a prosperous businessman. I don't know his private address, but his office is in Rutland House, in the City. Your people could look up the number, and ring him up there. I can't tell you much about the other nephew, Barry Benson, although I have met him."

"I've heard folk speak of Mr. Benson," said Docking. "But I didn't know that he was Mr. Hawken's nephew."

"It was probably Barry they meant," Paul replied. "He was here two or three months ago. It's a long time since Hubert has been to see his uncle. Too busy, I dare say. Barry has plenty of time on his hands, because he always seems to be out of a job. He's a rolling stone, who has tried pretty well everything, but never seems able to stay put. The last thing George told me about him was that he had taken to lorry driving. He didn't tell me the name of the firm he was working for, so he won't be easy to trace. We're nearly there now."

They turned a buttress of rock, and came suddenly into the widening of the ledge. George's shooting-stick, sketching block and pencil lay as Paul had seen them. Docking examined the edge of the ledge, thinking that a piece of it might have given way. But the solid rock showed no sign of fracture. He turned to Paul who was looking at the boldly pencilled outline on the sketching block.

"When did you last see Mr. Hawken alive, Mr. Clapdale?" Docking asked.

"As recently as yesterday morning," Paul replied. "Not here, but down by the harbour. He told me that he was playing with the idea of painting a picture of the fishing-boats, though that sort of thing wasn't really in his line."

"Was Mr. Hawken in his usual health and spirits?" Docking asked.

Paul shook his head at him. "Now don't you get it into your head that George pitched himself over. He would have been the last man in the world to do that. He was perfectly content with the life he led, and he had no worries. It's true that he hadn't a lot of money, but he didn't want it. He had enough for himself, and he had no one else to provide for. And he had no anxieties about the future. Sir Matthew, who is ten years older than George was, had told him that he had left him everything he possessed. George didn't commit suicide, you may be quite sure of that."

"Well, it'll be for a jury to decide," said Docking. "We must take Mr. Hawken's belongings back to the cottage."

Carrying these with them, they returned to the cottage, where Paul put them in the studio. Glancing round, he wondered what would become of the pictures. They would be put up for sale, he supposed, but surely they wouldn't fetch a lot. He rejoined Docking and they walked together to the village, where they parted.

As soon as Docking reached home, he rang up Superintendent Egford, in charge of the Thramsbury Division. Thramsbury was a market town, some five miles distant from Port Bosun. Egford listened to Docking's account of what had happened.

"Do you suspect foul play, Constable?" he asked. "I can't say that I do, sir," Docking replied. "There doesn't seem to be any motive. Mr. Hawken was well liked by everyone in Port Bosun. And theft can't have been the object."

"Mr. Hawken's relatives must be informed," said Egford. "Do you know anything of them?"

"I've been given the business address of one of them, sir," Docking replied. "Mr. Hubert Benson, Mr. Hawken's nephew. He has an office in Rutland House in the City."

"That's good enough," said Egford. "I'll get on to the City Police, and ask them to inform this Mr. Benson of his uncle's death. Then I'll look into things for myself. Stay where you are till I come."

Half an hour later Egford arrived in his car at the constable's house, where Docking made his report in detail.

"Who is this Mr. Clapdale?" Egford asked.

"He's a retired gentleman, sir," Docking replied. "He lives with his sister in a house called Merrymount, on the Thramsbury road. He and Mr. Hawken were great friends. I've often seen them together. It was he who gave Mr. Hubert Benson's office address."

"I've asked the City Police to contact Mr. Benson," said Egford. "And now I want to see the body."

He drove Docking to George's cottage. Docking unlocked the door, and they went in.

"You see the mark the doctor spoke of, sir," said Docking, as he drew back the sheet covering the body. "Mr. Clapdale says that he had never seen it when Mr. Hawken was alive."

Egford looked closely at the mark, which was certainly curious. A thin faint red line, running all round the dead man's neck. "Was Mr. Hawken wearing a tight collar when you recovered his body?" Egford asked.

Docking picked up the shirt which had been taken from George's body and displayed it. "He wasn't wearing a collar at all, sir," he replied. "Only this loose shirt."

"There's nothing tight about that," Egford remarked. "I don't see how a mark like that could have been made by a fall. It's a matter for the doctors to decide. Now you can show me where Mr. Hawken fell from."

They left the car where it was, and walked along the path to the ledge. Docking pointed out the spot where the shooting-stick and sketching block had been found.

"The doctor says that death took place about nine o'clock this morning, sir," he said. "Mr. Hawken must have been sitting here for some little while before then, because he had had time to begin a sketch. The body was seen lying on the flat rock below. The rock is covered now, because it's just about high water. But it would have been bare at nine o'clock."

Egford looked over the edge, to find that the sea was lapping against the face of the cliff.

"The question is, what caused Mr. Hawken to fall," he said. "He may have got up and walked to where I'm standing now. As he looked down, he had an attack of giddiness and lost his balance. You say that Mr. Clapdale is quite certain that his friend didn't commit suicide. That possibility can't be neglected, all the same. You knew Mr. Hawken, Constable. What's your opinion about that?"

"I hardly know, sir," Docking replied. "Mr. Clapdale says he had no worries, and I'm prepared to believe it."

"He lived by himself, you say?" Egford asked. "Loneliness sometimes drives people to suicide."

"I don't think that Mr. Hawken was lonely, sir," Docking replied. "It wasn't that he avoided people. It was just that he preferred to live alone. I've often seen him in the village talking to people. And he and Mr. Clapdale met nearly every day."

"People don't as a rule go suddenly off their heads," Egford remarked. "And that brings us to a third possibility. I don't altogether share your view that no foul play can have been involved. If Mr. Hawken was sitting here, intent upon what he was doing, anyone could have come upon him unawares. That person could have caught him by the shoulders, and tumbled him out of his seat and over the edge. What have you got to say to that, Constable?"

"I'd like to say this, sir," Docking replied. "That person must have known Mr. Hawken's habits, which means that he can't have been a stranger. And I'm quite sure that no one in Port Bosun would have murdered Mr. Hawken. What could they have to gain by it?"

"Well, you may be right," said Egford. "Keep your eyes and ears open, and see if you can pick up anything to throw a light on the matter. I must get back to Thramsbury."

They returned to the car. Egford gave Docking a lift to the village, then drove on to Thramsbury. When he reached the police station the sergeant on duty informed him that a message had just come through from the City Police. An inspector had been sent to Rutland House. Mr. Benson was not there, but his secretary had been interviewed. She had stated that Mr. Benson and his wife were in France, and were not expected back for a few days. The secretary could not tell the inspector where Mr. Benson was at the moment, as he had calls to make all over France. But she knew the name of a firm in Paris with which he was in close touch. She would write a letter to Mr. Benson, care of this firm, and she had no doubt that he would receive it with little delay.

Chapter II

The inquest was held on the afternoon of Friday, 16th June, in the Port Bosun village hall, the coroner sitting with a jury. The first witness called was Paul Clapdale. In the absence of any relative of the deceased, he gave evidence of identification. He had viewed the body, and recognised it as that of his friend George Hawken, single, aged seventy-five and living at Cliff Cottage, Port Bosun. The witness had last seen the deceased alive on Tuesday. He had then appeared to be in normal health and spirits. Paul then described how he had gone to look for the deceased on Wednesday morning. He had called at Cliff Cottage, and had found that the deceased was not at home. Guessing where he might be, he had gone along the ledge halfway up the cliff, and had seen the deceased lying on the flat rocks below. The tide was on the point of reaching the body.

Docking followed. At half-past three on Wednesday the last witness had called upon him and informed him of the circumstances. He had immediately taken steps to recover the body. Two of the Penwarne brothers had rowed him to the spot in their boat, and between them they had lifted the body from the water. The Penwarnes were not in court to give evidence, as they had gone out fishing in Seabird on Thursday's morning tide, and had not yet returned. The body had then been conveyed to Cliff Cottage.

The medical evidence was then taken. Dr. Godney described how he had visited Cliff Cottage at a quarter past four on Wednesday afternoon. He had there found the body of the deceased, with the clothing saturated. He had carried out an examination, and had found a fractured skull and a broken neck, besides other injuries. These were compatible with a fall from a height on to a hard surface. He had also found a reddish ring round the neck, for which he was unable to account. He had formed the opinion that death had occurred about nine o'clock on Wednesday morning.

Godney's place was taken by the county pathologist. With the assistance of the previous witness, he had examined the body of the deceased on Thursday morning. He had found the cause of death was the injuries received. Although when found the body had been submerged, death had not been due to drowning. He agreed with his colleagues that the injuries were such as might be expected to be caused by a fall from a height.

Asked by the coroner if he could account for the red ring round the neck, the witness replied that he was doubtful. It might have been produced by a cord being drawn tightly round the neck of the deceased. But the cause of death had certainly not been strangulation.

The coroner asked the witness what the immediate effect of a cord being drawn tightly round the neck would be. The reply was that the constriction would rapidly produce unconsciousness, but not immediate death. But in the case of the deceased, this was pure speculation. It was impossible to prove that the mark on the neck had actually been made by a cord. The deceased had died as the result of injuries received in his fall.

No further witnesses were called, and the coroner addressed the jury. They would no doubt be guided by the medical evidence in returning their verdict as to the cause of death. They would form their own opinion as to how the deceased came to fall from the cliff. They were at liberty to retire to consider their verdict.

The jury retired, and were absent for at least half an hour. When they returned, the coroner asked the foreman if they were agreed upon their verdict. The foreman replied that they were. They found that the death of the deceased had been due to the injuries he had received. But there was no evidence upon which they could base an opinion as to how and why he had fallen.

The coroner remarked that that amounted to an open verdict, and that he would record it as such. The usual formalities terminated the proceedings. Paul undertook to make the necessary arrangements for the funeral, and the coroner handed him the burial certificate. Upon that the court dispersed.

Egford had been present, seated at the coroner's table. It was clear to him that the prolonged absence of the jury showed that they had had some difficulty in arriving at their verdict. There might well have been a difference of opinion as to the cause of Mr. Hawken's fall. They had eventually agreed to return an open verdict.

Docking was in attendance, and Egford turned to him.

"Do many people go along that ledge, Constable?" he asked.

"Hardly anyone, sir," Docking replied. "It doesn't lead anywhere, and comes to an end about a hundred yards beyond where Mr. Hawken was sitting. There is a certain amount of traffic along the road which runs along the top of the cliffs. But very few people go along the ledge half-way down. If Mr. Hawken fell over about nine in the morning it is pretty certain that nobody else would have been on the ledge at that time."

"Where does the road lead to?" Egford asked.

"Nowhere in particular, sir," Docking replied. "It runs past a few farms, then comes out into the main road from Thramsbury to Westhaven. That road is narrow, winding and hilly. Most of the traffic along it goes to and from the farms. Any traffic between Port Bosun and Westhaven nearly always goes through Thramsbury."

"Do you think the verdict will be popular in Port Bosun?" Egford asked.

"Well, I don't know, sir," Docking replied. "Everybody knew Mr. Hawken and liked him, and I don't suppose the verdict will satisfy them. Several people have spoken to me about it in the last couple of days. None of them seem to believe that it was an accident, or that Mr. Hawken committed suicide. They've got it into their heads that he was done in.

"Have any of these people suggested to you who might have done him in?" Egford asked.

"No, sir, they haven't," Docking replied. "The way they look at it is that that's a job for the police. And one or two of them have said outright to my face that the police don't seem to be doing much about it."

"What do they expect us to do?" Egford demanded. "Some people are always ready to find fault with the police. Well, never mind, Constable. Stick to it, and perhaps you'll come upon some clue."

He drove back to Thramsbury, and when he reached the police station made a full report by telephone to the Chief Constable of the County.

"So the jury returned an open verdict," said the chief when Egford had finished. "That means that we've got to try to solve the mystery. Do your best, Superintendent. If you want any extra help, I'll arrange for you to have it."

"That's just it, sir," Egford replied. "Would you consider asking the Yard to help us?"

"The Yard?" the chief exclaimed. "Why, what could they do that you can't?"

"It's not that exactly, sir," Egford replied. "I'm told that the folk in Port Bosun don't think that the police are doing enough. If the Yard were called in, it might make a better impression."

"I see," said the chief. "If it's a question of saving face that's a different matter. Very well, then. I'll get on to the Yard and get them to send a man down. I'll say that he is to report to you."

So it came about that Inspector Arnold of the Criminal Investigation Department was dispatched to Thramsbury by the night train. Egford, who had been notified of his coming, met him on Saturday morning and drove him to the police station. Having given Arnold an outline of the case, Egford asked him what he would like to do first.

"Have breakfast," Arnold replied promptly. "I have never been able to work on an empty stomach."

"I haven't had breakfast myself yet," said Egford. "The Three Lions is only just over the way. Suppose we go there and have breakfast together."

Arnold replied that he would like nothing better. They went to the hotel and ordered breakfast. During the meal Egford gave Arnold some idea of Port Bosun.

"You'll find that it's no more than a fishing village, Mr. Arnold. There are no industries, and the only place of entertainment is a single cinema. Nor does Port Bosun pretend to be a resort. Some of the fishermen's wives let lodgings, and a few visitors may be found there in August. How they occupy their time I have never been able to discover."

Arnold smiled. "It doesn't sound exactly a Blackpool."

"It certainly isn't," Egford agreed. "But it is by no means so poverty stricken as you might suppose. Taking it all round, the fishermen do pretty well. They land their catches on the quay, where they are bought by the dealers. There is no railway nearer than here, so that the fish have to be carried by road."

"I gather from what you have told me that people who are not fishermen live in Port Bosun," Arnold remarked.

"Yes, but there aren't very many of them," Egford replied. "Most of the families have for generations earned their living by fishing. There are of course exceptions. Mostly retired folk, who have settled in Port Bosun for the sake of the peace and quiet they find there. Mr. Clapdale, whom I've told you about, and his sister are examples.

"I suppose the natives regard these immigrants as foreigners?" Arnold asked.

"I expect they do," Egford replied. "But it doesn't follow that they resent their presence. After all, the foreigners bring a certain amount of trade to the village. On the other hand, the natives are intensely clannish. Quarrel with one of them, and you'll find that you've quarrelled with the whole village."

The conversation continued until they had finished breakfast. "Now what, Mr. Arnold?" Egford asked.

"You tell me that Mr. Clapdale not only was the first to see the body but that he was a close friend of Mr. Hawken," Arnold replied. "I should like to see him, and get him to tell us what he can about Mr. Hawken's background. If you agree, that is."

"I quite agree," said Egford. "We'll go back to the police station and I'll ring up Merrymount, which is where Mr. Clapdale lives."

The call was put through, and Janet Clapdale answered it. She was sorry, but her brother was out. However, she was expecting him back any minute now. Yes, she was sure that he would be glad to see Mr. Egford and his friend.

Egford drove Arnold to Port Bosun. The road ran along the valley of the little river Bosun, with pasture land on either side. When they had reached the outskirts of the village, Egford pulled up at a gate bearing the name Merrymount. Beyond this a short drive led to a comparatively modern villa, surrounded by a garden. They alighted from the car and walked up the drive to the front door. Egford rang the bell, and the door was opened by Janet.

"Good morning, gentlemen," she said brightly. "My brother has just come in. I told him you were coming, and he's expecting you. Come in, and I'll take you to him."

She led them to a trim parlour in which Paul was sitting, smoking a pipe. He rose as they came in.

"I'm happy to meet you again, Mr. Egford," he said. "Will

you introduce your friend?"

"This is Inspector Arnold, from Scotland Yard." Egford replied.

"I am very pleased to meet you, Mr. Arnold," said Paul as they shook hands. "From Scotland Yard, indeed! I am very glad to hear it. You will no doubt be able to unravel the mystery of George's death. Do sit down, both of you. I'm sorry I can't offer you cigarettes, because we never seem to have any in the house. I never smoke them, and Janet doesn't smoke at all."

"May I be allowed to follow your example, and smoke my pipe?" Arnold asked.

"Why, of course!" Paul replied. Arnold filled his pipe, and Egford took a cigarette case from his pocket and lighted one from it.

"That's better," said Paul. "Now will you tell me what you have come to see me about?"

"You were, I understand, a close friend of Mr. Hawken?" Arnold replied.

"I may claim to have been that," said Paul. "My sister and I had known him ever since we came to Port Bosun seven years ago. I'll tell you how we first met George. I was on the point of retiring, and my sister was keeping house for me. We decided that we would leave Yorkshire, and spend the rest of our days in a warmer climate. We watched the advertisements in the newspapers, and saw one offering this house for sale, with immediate possession. We had neither of us ever heard of Port Bosun before, but we decided to have a look at the house.

"We went by train to Thramsbury, and put up at the Three Lions. Next day we called on the house agent who had inserted the advertisement He gave us full particulars of the house, and when we told him that we should like to see it, he gave us the key, apologising for not being able to show us the house himself, as he had a most urgent appointment that morning.

"We hired a car and driver, and drove to Port Bosun. At that time there was no name on the gate, and we passed the house without knowing it. As we reached the centre of the village an elderly gentleman came out of a shop. I called to him, and asked him if he could tell us the way to Merrymount. He said that he would be glad to show us where the house was, and I asked him into the car. On the way he told us that his name was George

Hawken, and that he had lived in Port Bosun all his life. I replied by telling him who we were, and that we wanted to look over Merrymount with a view to buying it if it suited us.

"We found that the house was the very thing we wanted. To cut a long story short, we bought it, and moved in a couple of months later. We had hardly settled down when George called on us. We were delighted to see him, and he was most helpful in telling us about the tradesmen in the village, and that sort of thing. He told us where he lived, and a day or two later I returned his call. From that time hardly a day passed that George and I did not meet. He seemed to enjoy my company, and I certainly enjoyed his."

"Mr. Hawken was a native of Port Bosun, I understand?" Arnold asked.

"He was indeed," Paul replied. "George told me that his family had owned fishing-boats here for generations. He said that they used to live in a house by the harbour, which was demolished when the quay was widened, many years ago. Both George and his elder brother broke away from the family tradition and took to painting. Matthew, Sir Matthew, as he became later, went to London, and made a name for himself as a portrait painter during the First War. George bought Cliff Cottage, and added a studio to it."

"Mr. George Hawken was not a rich man, I gather?" Arnold asked.

"Far from it," Paul replied. "He never became famous, as his brother did. He sold a picture or two now and again, but never at a high price. However, he did not complain. He told me that what he earned was sufficient for his needs. He was a man of very simple tastes, and never smoked or drank."

"Then we may take it that at the time of his death, Mr. Hawken was not in possession of much money?" Arnold suggested.

"Twenty-six pounds, fourteen shillings and threepence," Paul replied.

The promptitude of the answer astonished Arnold. "How do you know that, Mr. Clapdale?" he asked.

"Because I have counted the sum," Paul replied. "My action in so doing requires explanation. Some five years ago George made a will, and appointed his nephew Barry Benson and myself as his executors. He explained to us at the time that the will was a mere formality, as he had nothing to leave but Cliff Cottage and his pictures.

"The terms of the will are these. The cottage was to go to Barry, who was at liberty to sell it if he didn't want it. If Sir Matthew survived the testator, the pictures were to go to him. If Sir Matthew had died, the pictures were to be sold by auction, and the proceeds given to a local charity for the relief of necessitous fishermen. After deduction of funeral expenses, any cash in hand was to be given to the charity.

"As I have no idea where Barry is to be found, I felt it my duty to act on my sole responsibility, and yesterday I got Docking to admit me to the house. I knew where George kept his money, and in Docking's presence I counted it. Not wishing to leave the cash in the empty cottage, I took it away with me. I have it here now under lock and key. I may say that I have arranged for George to be buried this afternoon."

"Was Mr. Hawken in the habit of leaving the cottage unlocked when he went out?" Arnold asked.

"Always," Paul replied. "He never locked the door, even at night. He used to say that there was nothing in the cottage to tempt a burglar. And, for that matter, no one in Port Bosun would have taken anything of his. He was far too well liked for that."

"You are absolutely certain that Mr. Hawken had no enemy in the village?" Arnold asked.

"As certain as I can be," Paul replied. "As I said a few minutes ago the natives are intensely clannish, and George was one of them. They may bicker among themselves, but their bickering never amounts to more than a family squabble. I quite understand the drift of your question, Mr. Arnold. I can only say that if George's death was due to foul play, I am convinced that no one in Port Bosun was guilty."

"Admitting the possibility of foul play, have you any theory, Mr. Clapdale?" Arnold asked.

Paul shook his head. "None whatever. A murderer must necessarily expect to gain something by his crime. But who could have expected to gain anything from George's death? On the other hand, I am firmly convinced that George did not commit suicide."

"Then only accident remains," said Arnold. "Can you form any idea of how such an accident can have happened?"

"I find it very difficult to do so," Paul replied. "The situation must have been this. George was sitting on his shooting-stick with the sketching block on his knees. I have often seen him sitting like that when he was sketching. There can be no question of his having slipped off the stick and fallen over the edge. The stick and sketching block were lying well away from the edge, six feet or more. I can only suppose that for some reason or other George laid the block aside and got up. The point of the stick would not have penetrated the rock, so it fell on its side. George walked to the edge, perhaps to get a better view of what he was sketching. While he was standing there, he lost his balance and fell."

"That is by no means impossible," Arnold agreed. "But we cannot eliminate the possibility of foul play. Can you tell us if there was any animosity between Mr. Hawken and his relatives?"

"I am sure there was not," Paul replied. "George and his brother were devoted to each other. George always spoke of Sir Matthew in the most affectionate terms. And it is known that Sir Matthew has made a will leaving everything to his brother."

"And how did the two nephews and their uncle get on?" Arnold asked.

"Again, there was no animosity," Paul replied. "Of the two, George preferred Barry, of whom he was genuinely fond. Barry has often been here to see his uncle. Although George admired Hubert for the way he had got on in the world, I don't think that he had any great affection for him. Of Hubert I know nothing beyond what George told me, for I have never met him. So far as I know, he has not been to Port Bosun while I have been living here."

"Did Mr. Hawken ever visit his relations?" Arnold asked.

"Very rarely," Paul replied. "And then only to see his brother. George spent a couple of days with Sir Matthew last summer. When he came back he told me that though his brother was an invalid who could only get about in a wheeled chair, he seemed otherwise astonishingly fit for a man of his age. Sir Matthew must be eighty-five at least. I am afraid that the news of George's death will be a great shock to him."

"I should tell you this, Mr. Clapdale," said Egford. "The police have taken steps to get in touch with Mr. Hubert Benson. They have learnt that he is or was in France on business. A letter has been sent to him there."

"It will be Hubert's business to break the news to Sir Matthew," Paul replied. "One can only hope that he will do so as gently as possible. Is there anything else you would like to ask me?"

Arnold rose to his feet, and Egford followed his example. "No, thank you, Mr. Clapdale," said Arnold. "We are very grateful to you for what you have told us. We need not trouble you any further."

Paul saw his visitors to the door, and they seated themselves in the car. "I should like to see the ledge from which Mr. Hawken fell," said Arnold.

"I was going to suggest that you should do that," Egford replied. As they drove through the village he pointed out to Arnold the various objects of interest. They followed the road to where the path branched off and alighted.

"It's only a short walk from here," said Egford.

In a few minutes they reached the spot where the ledge widened. "This is where the shooting-stick and sketching block were found," said Egford. "And the body was lying on the flat rocks immediately below."

Arnold looked over the edge. "A tidy fall," he remarked. "I see the rocks are uncovered now. Were they like that when Mr. Hawken fell?"

"They must have been much as they are now," Egford replied. "At nine o'clock on Wednesday morning the tide was well out. By the time the body was recovered it had risen, and the rocks were covered to a depth of about two feet."

"The body lay there all day without being seen," said Arnold. "Wasn't that rather extraordinary?"

"Apparently not," Egford replied. "I'm told that very few people walk along this ledge. And the body wouldn't have been visible from the top of the cliff. The protruding ledge would hide it."

"Well, how did it happen?" Arnold asked. "I'm inclined to rule out the theory of suicide. Mr. Clapdale, who seems to have known Mr. Hawken very well, is convinced that he would not have taken his own life. Apart from that, it seems to me that if Mr. Hawken had intended to throw himself over the cliff, he wouldn't have sat down and begun a sketch before he did so.

"Then we come to accident, which I find not easy to explain. Mr. Clapdale may be right. Mr. Hawken lost his balance while he was looking over the edge. But why should he have looked over the edge? And, if he did so, what made him lose his balance? He didn't drink, so a drop too much didn't account for it."

"The only alternative is that Mr. Hawken was pushed over," Egford remarked. "And if that was the case, who pushed him?"

"We shall have to leave the question of who out of it for the present," Arnold replied. "But I think I see how it could have been done. While we were on our way here I noticed that we came upon this spot quite suddenly, owing to the bend in the ledge. Mr. Hawken, sitting here could not have seen a person advancing along the ledge until he was only a few feet away. And if Mr. Hawken was looking in the opposite direction he might well have been taken by surprise.

"Now we come to that strange red mark on Mr. Hawken's neck. The pathologist said that it might have been caused by a cord drawn tightly round the neck. Perhaps it was. The person I have imagined crept up behind Mr. Hawken, dropped a loop of cord over his head, and pulled hard on both the ends. Again according to the pathologist, unconsciousness would have resulted very rapidly. Being unconscious, Mr. Hawken was incapable of offering resistance. His assailant removed the cord, and rolled the body over the cliff."

"How did your imaginary person know where Mr. Hawken was to be found?" Egford asked.

"I can think of an answer to that question," Arnold replied. "The person expected to find Mr. Hawken at home in the morning. He went in the direction of Cliff Cottage, having with him a length of cord. As he approached the cottage, Mr. Hawken came out, carrying his stick and sketching block. The person watched the direction in which Mr. Hawken went, keeping out of his sight.

"Mr. Hawken had time to reach the ledge and begin a sketch. Why did not the person follow him at once? Perhaps because, the cottage being empty, he took the opportunity of entering it. It may have contained something which the person wished to acquire. He may or may not have found this. At all events an interval elapsed before he followed Mr. Hawken and murdered him."

"That theory is plausible enough," said Egford. "But the murderer's motive still remains obscure."

"Mr. Clapdale says that nobody gains anything by Mr. Hawken's death," Arnold replied. "But that isn't strictly true. The nephew to whom Cliff Cottage was left benefits to the extent of its value. It seems to me that our job is to find out where Barry Benson was on Wednesday morning."

Chapter III

Desmond Merrion was in London that week-end. He was sitting in his rooms in St. James's on Sunday afternoon when his telephone rang. He answered the call, giving his name.

"This is Arnold, speaking from the Yard," came the reply. "Can I come and have a chat with you, if you're not too busy?"

"Come along by all means," said Merrion. "You'll find me alone."

Half an hour later Arnold arrived. "Well, and what have you come to see me about?" Merrion asked, as the two old friends settled themselves down. "Is it that you have an interesting case on hand?"

"It's a case that may interest you," Arnold replied. "I was at a little place called Port Bosun yesterday. Have you ever heard of it?"

"I've heard of it, but I've never been there," said Merrion. "It's a fishing village not far from Thramsbury, I believe."

"That's right," Arnold replied. "I was sent there to investigate the death of a Mr. George Hawken, who was killed in a fall from a cliff. He was an artist."

"George Hawken, an artist?" Merrion asked. "I know of Sir Matthew Hawken, who had a great reputation as an artist in his time. Long ago he painted a portrait of Mavis. You've seen it hanging in the dining-room at High Eldersham Hall."

"Sir Matthew is Mr. George Hawken's brother," Arnold replied. "There are two nephews of the name of Benson. Do you know anything about either of them?"

Merrion shook his head. "Nothing. I have never spoken to Sir Matthew, though I have seen him from a distance. He lives in what amounts to a moated castle, complete with drawbridge. I know that, because the parson of the parish is an old friend of mine, and I go and see him sometimes."

"What is the name of the parish?" Arnold asked.

"Shepherd Green," Merrion replied. "And Sir Matthew's place is called Moat Barn. Now tell me about the death of his brother."

Arnold told his story in detail. "Here you have the case of a man living alone and given to sitting and sketching in a solitary spot," he went on. "I'm pretty well satisfied that he didn't commit suicide. It seems unlikely that he fell off the ledge by accident. Was he first rendered unconscious and then pushed over? The general opinion in the village seems to favour foul play."

"And what is your own opinion?" Merrion asked.

"I'm inclined to think that Mr. Hawken was murdered," Arnold replied. "That mark round his neck seems to me to be highly significant. But the motive is not easy to understand. Mr. Hawken possessed nothing of value except his cottage and his pictures. The pictures he left to his brother, and the cottage to his nephew Barry Benson. Is it possible that his nephew murdered him for the sake of the cottage?"

"It isn't impossible," Merrion replied. "Men have been murdered for the sake of things of far less value than that. What do you know of this nephew?"

"Precious little," said Arnold. "He seems to be a ne'er-do-well, always sliding out of one job and getting another. I suppose that's not difficult in these days of full employment. At present he is said to be driving a lorry for a long distance haulage firm."

"You are taking steps to trace him, I suppose?" Merrion asked.

"Naturally," Arnold replied. "I have drafted a circular to be sent to all police forces in the country, asking them to contact all the long distance haulage firms in their area and inquire whether any of them employ a driver of the name of Barry Benson. Tomorrow, Wighton, whom you have met, is to go round all the firms in the London area, asking the same question. We're bound to get the fellow."

Merrion smiled. "And if you do? You have no evidence so far that he murdered his uncle. Or, for that matter, that Mr. Hawken was murdered, though I agree with you that he probably was. When you've laid hands on Barry Benson it will be interesting to hear what he has to say for himself."

Arnold stayed with Merrion for a cup of tea, then returned to Scotland Yard, where he occupied himself with other matters. On Monday morning Detective-Sergeant Wighton set out on his round of inquiries. He had made a list of the long distance haulage firms in the London area and he called on these in turn.

In the middle of the afternoon he reached the premises of Messrs. Aspall and Sons. He produced his credentials and was shown into the presence of the manager.

"Well, Sergeant, and what can I do for you?" the manager asked.

"We're looking for a man called Barry Benson," Wighton replied. "Do you employ a driver of that name?"

"Eh?" the manager exclaimed. "So it's come to that, has it? We did employ a driver of that name, but it seems that we have ceased to do so. What do the police know about Benson, may I ask?"

"Very little," Wighton replied. "We want to find him, that's all."

"I can't tell you where he is," said the manager. "All I know is that he has disappeared."

"When did you last see him?" Wighton asked.

"Last Tuesday afternoon," the manager replied. "This was the way of it. For some time past we have had a contract to convey consignments of Danish bacon from Milwall Dock to a place called Thramsbury. For that purpose we always use a big van. Last Tuesday a consignment was ready at the dock, and on communicating with our agent at Thramsbury, he told us that the van could pick up a return load of vegetables for Covent Garden.

"That afternoon Benson came to see me. The regular driver of the van was sick, and Benson told me that the man who had taken his place didn't know the way to Thramsbury. Benson said that he knew the district well, and offered to take over the van for the trip, while the other man took over his lorry. I agreed to that. Benson loaded up the bacon, and brought the van back here. He was due to start for Thramsbury about midnight. He must have done so, for the consignment was delivered on Wednesday morning.

"The vegetables were to be picked up at a place called Westhaven on Wednesday evening and to be delivered at Covent Garden on Thursday morning. And that's where the trouble started. On Thursday morning our Thramsbury agent rang up and said that the vegetables had not been collected. The van was all ready, but the driver couldn't be found."

"Has nothing been heard of Benson since then?" Wighton

asked.

"Not by us or by our Thramsbury agent," the manager replied. "We sent another man down there by train on Thursday. He loaded up the vegetables that evening, and delivered them at Covent Garden next morning. They were of course a day late, and the people who consigned them were very much upset about it. It will end by our having to pay them compensation."

"Did you consider Benson to be a reliable man?" Wighton asked.

"I had always found him a reliable and steady driver," the manager replied. "He hadn't been with us more than a few months but he seemed to have settled down quite happily. Why he should have taken himself off like that is more than I can understand. I shouldn't have expected him to let us down so badly."

"Can you tell me where Benson lives?" Wighton asked.

"He lodges in this very street," the manager replied. "But you won't find him there. His landlady came here this morning to ask if we knew what had become of her lodger. She had last seen him on Tuesday, when he slept in her house after he'd had his supper until nearly midnight. She wondered whether it was because he owed her money that he hadn't come back."

Wighton entered in his note-book the number of Benson's lodging, and the name and address of the firm's agent in Thramsbury. Then after promising the manager that he would let him know if the police obtained any news of Benson, he took his departure. Then he went straight back to Scotland Yard, where he asked if Arnold would see him.

Arnold was very ready to see him, and Wighton went up to his room. He repeated his conversation with the manager to which Arnold listened with the greatest interest.

"It's as plain as a pikestaff!" Arnold exclaimed when Wighton had come to an end. "Benson wanted to get to Port Bosun. That's why he took on the job of driving the van to Thramsbury. All right, Sergeant. Keep in touch with Aspall and Sons, just in case Benson goes back to them. Not that I think it in the least likely that he will."

Wighton went out, and Arnold put a call through to Egford. "I've got some news for you," he said. "It's too long a story to tell you on the telephone. I'll come down by the night train as before, and perhaps you'll be good enough to meet me."

Egford promised to do that, and Arnold rang off. That evening he caught the train and reached Thramsbury on Tuesday morning. Egford met him and took him to the Three Lions, and as they were having breakfast Arnold told him of the information obtained by Wighton.

"The manager told Wighton that the firm's agents here were Saxthorpe Brothers, of River Street," Arnold concluded.

"I know them, of course," Egford replied. "The two Saxthorpe Brothers own a garage and repair shop. They are motor engineers, and they do a certain amount of local haulage as well. When you're ready, we'll go along to their place. We're sure to find one of the brothers there."

When they had finished breakfast, they drove through the town to River Street. Egford pulled up outside an extensive yard, at one side of which was a range of buildings. As they stopped a middle-aged man came out of one of these.

"That's Cyril Saxthorpe, the elder brother," said Egford. "Come along, and I'll introduce you."

Seeing Arnold and Egford alight from the car, Saxthorpe came towards them. "Good morning, Superintendent," he said. "Can I do anything for you?"

"We've come to get some information from you, Mr. Saxthorpe," Egford replied. "This is my friend Inspector Arnold, from Scotland Yard."

"Scotland Yard, eh?" said Saxthorpe. "That sounds as if someone was in for trouble. Not us, I hope?"

"Not at all," Arnold replied. "Our inquiries concern a driver employed by Aspall and Sons, who was here last week."

"That confounded fellow?" Saxthorpe exclaimed. "He's given us more trouble and worry than we've had for a long time. Come into the office, and I'll tell you what I can about him."

He led them across the yard to the buildings. In one of them was a comfortable little office, where they sat down.

"Now you shall hear the story," said Saxthorpe. "On Wednesday morning of last week I was in this room early because I was expecting one of Aspalls' vans with a load of bacon for a wholesale grocer in the town. At about half-past seven the van drove into the yard, and I went to meet it. The driver was a man whom I did not know. I asked him his name, and he told me it was Benson. He said that the regular driver was sick, and that he had taken over the job.

"Before I go any further, I should explain that we have a rest-room for long distance drivers and that there is a cafe over the way where they can get a meal. I told Benson about this and asked him if he would like some breakfast and a sleep afterwards. One of our chaps would drive the van to the wholesale grocers' place and see to its being unloaded. Benson thanked me and went off in the direction of the cafe.

"I didn't see him again until about noon, by which time the van had been unloaded and was back in the yard here. Benson came to see me and asked what about the vegetables he was to load up. I told him he couldn't do anything till six o'clock. Then he would have to drive to Juniper Farm, on the outskirts of Westhaven. He would find the vegetables ready there, and the farm chaps would load them up. When they'd done that, he could start back for Covent Garden. Benson said that he had had a good sleep. He would get his lunch at the cafe and then have a look round the town.

"Six o'clock came, but Benson did not appear. I cursed his unpunctuality and waited. Time passed, but still no Benson. I didn't know what to do. Although our chaps were quite capable of driving the van about the town, none of them would have taken on the job of driving it to London. They had no experience of long distance work. Besides Aspalls wouldn't have liked their van to be taken over by any driver but one of their own. At eight o'clock I rang up Juniper Farm and told them that the vegetables could not be collected that evening. As you may imagine, they were not best pleased to hear that."

"And you never saw Benson again?" Arnold asked. "Not a shadow of him," Saxthorpe replied. "On Thursday morning, as early as I thought there would be someone in the office, I rang up Aspalls and told them what had happened. They sent one of their drivers down by train. He took over the van and went to Juniper Farm. But a whole day had been wasted, and that hadn't improved the vegetables. Where Benson had gone off to and why I can't imagine. Since you gentlemen are inquiring about him, am I to gather that he is wanted by the police?"

"We're anxious to question him," Arnold replied. "Did he happen to mention that he knew anyone in these parts?"

"He told me that he knew where Juniper Farm was," said Saxthorpe. "So he must have been here before. But he didn't tell me that he knew anybody. If I ever see him again, I'll give him a piece of my mind."

"We'll do our best to find him," Arnold replied. "We're very much obliged to you for what you've told us, Mr. Saxthorpe. We won't waste any more of your time."

He and Egford went back to the car and drove to the police station, where they went to the superintendent's room. Egford opened a drawer of his desk and took from it a bus time-table, which he studied for a moment.

"A bus leaves here at eight-fifteen in the morning and reaches Port Bosun at eight-forty," he said. "Does that suggest anything to you, Mr. Arnold?"

"It does indeed," Arnold replied. "What time is the next bus from Port Bosun?"

"A bus leaves there at nine forty-five," said Egford. "It gets here at ten-ten."

"Then I think that we can reconstruct events," Arnold replied. "Benson arrived with the van at half-past seven. Mr. Saxthorpe saw him go off. Where does the bus start from?"

"The market place," said Egford. "Benson would have to pass the cafe in order to get there."

"And that, no doubt, is what he did," said Arnold. "He caught the bus and reached Port Bosun at twenty minutes to nine. It wouldn't have taken him ten minutes to walk to Cliff Cottage. He went in, but his uncle wasn't there. He guessed that he was out sketching, and had a pretty good idea where he might be. He went to look for him, and came upon him unawares. He dropped the cord over Mr. Hawken's head and pulled it tight. Then he rolled him over the edge.

"Having done what he had set out to do, he caught the next bus back here. For the next couple of hours he kept out of the way. Then he presented himself to Mr. Saxthorpe, on the pretext of getting his instructions. That was the last time he was seen in this town. No doubt he cleared out immediately afterwards."

"I expect that was the way of it," Egford agreed. "But I don't understand why he showed himself to Saxthorpe. Why didn't he make himself scarce as soon as he got back here?"

"Perhaps he meant to create the impression that he had

been asleep in the rest-room," Arnold replied. "The question is, how are we going to verify Benson's movements on Wednesday morning? The bus conductor couldn't help us. He wouldn't remember what passengers he had carried on any particular morning last week. No doubt Benson was seen in Port Bosun, but it is most unlikely that he was recognised."

"You're right there, Mr. Arnold," said Egford. "I'll tell the constable at Port Bosun to make inquiries. But I don't think it's likely that he'll get any information. Where do you suppose Benson bolted to?"

"London, I expect," Arnold replied. "It's the best place to hide up in. But Benson certainly didn't go back to Stepney. By this time he'll have got himself a job in another part of town, probably under a false name. I'll get a description of him from Aspalls and circulate it."

"If he went to London, that may explain why he hung about here for so long," said Egford. "There's a train from here to London at twelve-thirty. Possibly he travelled by that."

"He probably did," Arnold replied. "Now, don't you think it would be a good thing for us to have a word with Mr. Clapdale?"

Egford agreed, and they drove to Merrymount. Paul was at home and welcomed them cordially. "What can I do for you gentlemen?" he asked.

"You can give us your opinion, Mr. Clapdale," Arnold replied. "Barry Benson was in this neighbourhood last Wednesday, and could have been in Port Bosun at nine o'clock in the morning."

A look of amazement spread over Paul's face. "Barry here?" he exclaimed. "You can't surely mean that he had anything to do with George's death?"

"It is possible that he may have," Arnold replied. "And what lends colour to that possibility is the fact that he has disappeared. These are the facts." He told Paul the story in brief. "Now, what do you think, Mr. Clapdale?" he concluded.

"I can't understand it," Paul replied. "Why should Barry have murdered his uncle? What had he to gain by George's death?"

"The cottage," said Arnold. "You told us that Mr. Hawken had left it to him. Benson owed money to his landlady, which seems to show that he was in a bad way financially."

"If he was, he could have raised money without committing murder," Paul replied. "He could have applied to his brother Hubert, or to his Uncle Matthew. For that matter, I would have helped him out myself."

"Perhaps he had already approached his brother and his uncle, and neither of them would give him what he asked," said Arnold.

"That may be," Paul agreed. "George told me that neither of them had much use for Barry. They considered him something of a disgrace to the family. In their opinion he ought to have found himself a good job and stuck to it."

The conversation continued for a little while longer. Then Arnold and Egford left Merrymount and drove back to Thramsbury, whence Arnold took a train back to London. On Wednesday morning he told Wighton to get a description of Barry Benson, and to circulate it to all the metropolitan divisions.

Then he took the Underground to the City, and called at Rutland House. A notice-board in the hall informed him that the offices of Benson &Co., Import and Export Merchants, were on the second floor. He went up in the lift, and found a door on which was the name of the firm and the word "Inquiries." He knocked on the door, and a female voice bade him enter. He did so, and a girl who was working at a desk rose and approached him.

"What can I do for you?" she asked pleasantly.

Arnold produced his card and showed it to her. "Can I speak to Mr. Hubert Benson?" he replied.

"I will go and ask him," said the girl. She opened an inner door and passed through. In a minute or two she returned. "Mr. Benson will see you. Will you come this way, please?"

She ushered Arnold into an office where Hubert Benson was sitting. He was a man in the forties, with sharp features and a business-like expression.

"Come in and sit down, Inspector," he said brusquely. "May I ask what brings you here?"

"I am in search of information, Mr. Benson," Arnold replied. "Have you seen your brother Barry recently?"

Hubert shook his head. "No, I haven't. Barry and I don't see much of each other these days. He flits from one job to another, and I am too busy with my own affairs to go chasing after him."

"Your brother has not been asking you for money?" Arnold asked.

"No, he hasn't," Hubert replied. "He knows that it would be no good. I shouldn't give him any money if he asked me for it. It would only be throwing it down the drain. What has Barry been up to that makes you interested in him?"

"We don't know that he has been up to anything," said Arnold. "Except that he left his job very suddenly last week. But we believe that he may have seen Mr. George Hawken shortly before his death."

"Poor old Uncle George!" Hubert exclaimed. "It was a great shock to me when I heard about it. I was in France at the time. My business frequently takes me to the Continent. My secretary wrote to tell me about it, but as I had no fixed address, her letter did not reach me until Saturday afternoon."

"You came back to England on receipt of that letter?" Arnold asked.

"I flew to England that evening," Hubert replied. "My concern was for my Uncle Matthew. I knew that he would be deeply distressed by his brother's death, and I felt that I ought at least to offer him my sympathy. I drove down to Moat Barn on Sunday, and found to my astonishment that Uncle Matthew had not heard the news. I cannot understand how it was that he had not been informed."

"It was thought best that one of his family should break the news to Sir Matthew," said Arnold.

"That fell to my lot," Hubert replied. "I broke it to him as gently as I could, and he was, as I had feared, greatly distressed. I told him all I knew, which was that Uncle George had died suddenly as the result of an accident. Perhaps you can give me further particulars, Inspector?"

"Your uncle had been sketching not far from Cliff Cottage on Wednesday morning," said Arnold. "That afternoon his friend Mr. Clapdale saw his body lying on the rocks at the foot of the cliff. Steps were taken to recover it, and an inquest was held on Friday. The verdict was that your uncle had died as a result of the injuries received in his fall, but that there was no evidence to show how he had fallen."

"It was, of course, an accident," Hubert replied. "Uncle

George would never have committed suicide. Well, Inspector, you'll realise that I'm a busy man. I'm sorry that I can't give you any information about Barry. If he comes to see me, I'll let you know. Good morning."

Chapter IV

Days passed, and still Barry Benson had not been traced. It occurred to Arnold that he might have taken refuge with his Uncle Matthew, though that did not seem very likely. However, Arnold felt that he ought not to neglect any possibility. On the Monday following his visit to Rutland House, he took a police car and drove to Shepherd Green. On reaching the village he inquired of a passer-by as to the whereabouts of Moat Barn. The man pointed. "That's the place you want," he replied.

The village stood at the edge of an expanse of marshland. In the centre of this rose a mound, on which stood a building which appeared to be a vast barn. Arnold thanked the man, and drove along a track across the marsh. This ran between deep and wide ditches on either side, cuts, as they were called locally. When he reached the mound, Arnold found that one of these cuts completely surrounded it, forming what was in fact a moat. There was no fixed bridge over the cut, but on the mound side of it a wooden platform was drawn up. Arnold remembered Merrion's description of Moat Barn. This no doubt was the drawbridge.

From the moat the mount rose gently to a flat top. On this was the barn, now converted into a dwelling-house. This was surrounded partly by a garden and partly by stone paving. A wide path ran spirally from the drawbridge to the door of the house.

Since no one was visible, Arnold told the driver to sound his horn. He did so, but for some minutes this produced no result. Then the drawbridge began to move. It slanted from the vertical and at last came to rest on the outer bank of the moat. A man wearing an apron appeared and crossed the bridge to the car. "Have you an appointment with Sir Matthew?" he asked.

"I have no appointment," Arnold replied. "But I have come here to call upon Sir Matthew."

The man shook his head. "I doubt whether Sir Matthew will see you. He very rarely sees anyone without an appointment."

Arnold produced his card and showed it to him. "He will

hardly refuse to see a police officer?"

The man looked at the card. "Well, I don't know, I'm sure," he replied hesitatingly. "I think you had better see Miss Paris. She's indoors. I'll show you the way."

Arnold alighted from the car, and followed the man across the bridge and up the path. When they reached the door of the house, the man opened it without ceremony.

"A police officer to see you, miss," he announced. When Arnold had entered, he shut the door and made off.

Arnold found himself in a vast studio, hung with paintings. At one side of it stood a four-poster bed, and on the other side was a gallery. There were several arm-chairs set about the studio, and in one of these sat a young woman wearing a nurse's uniform. Arnold's first impression of her was that she ought to have been a film star. The prim uniform seemed a mockery when worn by one with her face and figure.

She rose as Arnold came in. "I am Sir Matthew's nurse," she said. "Will you tell me what the police want with me?"

Arnold told her his name and where he came from. "I hoped to see Sir Matthew Hawken," he went on. "Do you think he would consent to speak to me?"

"I would rather he were not disturbed," she replied. "Couldn't you tell me what it is you want? As well as nursing Sir Matthew, I look after his affairs for him."

"Then I will ask you a question, Miss Paris," said Arnold. "Is Mr. Barry Benson here?"

The young woman shook her head. "There is no one here but Sir Matthew, myself, and Albert Oakley, the man who let you in just now."

"Has Mr. Barry Benson been here lately?" Arnold asked.

"He came here one Sunday afternoon, three weeks ago yesterday," she replied. "But Sir Matthew wouldn't see him. I think he guessed why Mr. Barry had come here. Sir Matthew was sitting in his wheeled chair on the terrace, as he is now. When I told him that Mr. Barry was here, he said that I was to send him about his business."

"And did you?" Arnold asked.

"Not until he'd told me what he'd come about," she replied. "He said that he was desperately short of money, and that he had hoped that his uncle would have given him some. He had spent all his money backing greyhounds, and none of them had won. He was so short that he couldn't pay his landlady, and if he didn't manage to do that somehow, she would turn him out. I asked him how much he owed her, and he said four pounds. I have some money of my own, and I gave him four pounds out of that. But I warned him that I should never do such a thing again. I've never told Sir Matthew that I gave Mr. Barry anything. I should only let myself in for a scolding if I did."

"You have heard nothing of Mr. Barry since Mr. George Hawken's death?" Arnold asked.

"Nothing whatever," she replied. "It was Mr. Barry's brother, Mr. Hubert, who told us about that. He had been in France when it happened, but as soon as he heard the news he flew back and drove down here. He told us that his Uncle George had had a fatal accident, but that he didn't know the details."

"Was his brother's death a great blow to Sir Matthew?" Arnold asked.

"It was indeed," she replied. "As soon as Sir Matthew realised the truth he collapsed. I sent Albert for Dr. Kent. He came at once, and after a while he got Sir Matthew round. But for the next two or three days Sir Matthew didn't feel strong enough to get out of bed, and I had the greatest difficulty in getting him to eat anything. But I'm glad to say that the shock seems to be wearing off. What is worrying Sir Matthew now is the matter of his will."

"I understand that Sir Matthew had made a will in his brother's favour?" said Arnold.

"Not entirely," she replied. "He had left very generous legacies to both Albert and myself. The balance of his money and his collection of pictures he left to Mr. George."

"The collection is of considerable value, I expect?" Arnold asked.

Miss Paris nodded. "Very considerable. Sir Matthew is not only an artist himself, but an excellent judge of art. In his earlier days, long before I knew him, he had an almost uncanny gift for spotting artists whose work would become popular. He would buy their pictures before they became known, then sell them again when the artists had established their names. But he hasn't sold them all yet. There are pictures hanging in this studio which must be almost priceless."

"And who will the pictures go to now?" Arnold asked. "To one or both of Sir Matthew's nephews, perhaps?"

Miss Paris smiled. "I don't think that's very likely. Sir Matthew has not yet made up his mind what is to become of them. He talks about leaving them to the Tate Gallery. He realises that he will have to make a fresh will. He has gone so far as to burn his existing one. But his lawyer, Mr. Bridgwater, is away on a cruise, and will not be back until next month. Sir Matthew says that the new will can well wait till then."

Affixed to the outer door of the studio was a heavy brass knocker, in the form of a dolphin. As she finished speaking this sounded, not loudly. "Excuse me, Mr. Arnold," said Miss Paris. She went to the door and opened it. "Come in, both of you!" she exclaimed. "Sir Matthew is sitting on the terrace. He'll be glad to see you, I'm sure."

"We saw the drawbridge down, so we came up," was the reply. "I met the doctor in the village. He said he was coming here, and offered me a lift. I hope we're not intruding?"

"Of course not," she replied. "I'll take you to see Sir Matthew, Doctor. Do you mind waiting here for a few minutes, Mr. Dedham?"

Arnold rose as a middle-aged man in clerical garb entered the room. "My name is Luke Dedham, and I'm the parson of the parish," he said. "I didn't know that there was a visitor here, though I might have guessed it, because I saw a car standing in the road. I don't think that we've met before?"

"I'm sure we haven't," Arnold replied. "This is the first time that I have been here. My name is Arnold, and I am an officer of the C.I.D. But although we have not met until now, we have, I believe, a mutual friend. Desmond Merrion, of High Eldersham Hall."

"Why, of course!" Dedham exclaimed. "Desmond has often spoken to me of you. Have you seen him lately?"

"About a fortnight ago," Arnold replied. "He was in London for the week-end, and I went to see him. He told me then that you and he met sometimes."

"So we do," said Dedham. "And we hope to meet again very soon. I have asked him and Mavis to stay at the vicarage for our cricket week, which opens here on the tenth of next month. Desmond has been a very fine cricketer in his time, and I'm going to make him play for Shepherd Green. He says his cricketing days are over, but I think I shall be able to persuade him. Are you a cricketer yourself, Mr. Arnold?"

Arnold shook his head. "People in my walk of life don't have much time to play cricket. The most we can hope for is to snatch an hour or so to watch a match."

They were still talking about cricket when Miss Paris reappeared, accompanied by Dr. Kent, to whom Arnold was introduced. Shortly afterwards Arnold took his leave. As he started down the path, an elderly man was coming up it. He was wearing a smock, a big straw hat, and a long sacking apron. Arnold took him to be the gardener.

On his way back to London, Arnold considered what he had seen and heard. He had failed to locate Barry, who had not taken refuge at Moat Barn. Or had he? Was that dazzling young woman to be trusted? Unknown to Sir Matthew, she might be concealing Barry, if not in Moat Barn itself, then somewhere in Shepherd Green. It was probable that when he had called that Sunday, she had helped him out of his difficulties. It was even possible that for some time there had been an understanding between them.

Upon one point there could be no doubt. Barry had been in financial difficulties. He had endeavoured to approach his Uncle Matthew, but had been refused an audience. Miss Paris had taken pity on him, but the sum she had given him wouldn't have carried him very far. Failing Uncle Matthew, he had decided to appeal to Uncle George. He had taken over the job of driving the van to Thramsbury because that would provide him with an opportunity of doing so.

At this stage in his reasoning an idea occurred to Arnold. As soon as he reached Scotland Yard he telephoned through to Egford, telling him to expect him next day at the usual time. He travelled by the night train, and found Egford on Thramsbury platform. "Good morning, Mr. Arnold," said Egford. "It's pleasant to see you again so soon. Have you any news of that young rascal Barry Benson?"

"None, I'm afraid," Arnold replied. "I went down to Sir Matthew Hawken's place yesterday, but I was told that Barry wasn't there. When we've had breakfast, do you think I could drive to Port Bosun and call on Mr. Clapdale?"

Egford had no objection to this. They had breakfast at the Three Lions, then drove to Merrymount. Janet Clapdale opened the door to them. No, she was sorry that her brother was not at home. He had gone to Cliff Cottage to see about packing up Mr. Hawken's pictures. He had taken a man from the furniture removers with him.

Arnold thanked her, and he and Egford drove to Cliff Cottage. As they alighted from the car, Paul and a man with a bowler hat came out of the cottage door. "You'll get on with the job as soon as you can, won't you?" Paul asked.

"Certainly, Mr. Clapdale," the man replied. "I'll get the pictures packed to-morrow, and as soon as you let me have the address, I'll send them off."

The man started towards the village, and Paul turned to his visitors. "Those pictures have been very much on my mind," he said. "I should like Sir Matthew to have them as soon as possible, but the trouble is that I don't know his address. I have written to Hubert Benson asking him for it, but I haven't had a reply yet."

"I can give it to you," Arnold replied. "May we go in and talk to you, Mr. Clapdale?"

"Of course," Paul replied. He led them into the kitchen, where the three of them sat down. "You told us that you had taken charge of what money there was in the house," said Arnold. "Did you have to search for it, or did you know where to find it?"

"I knew where to find it," Paul replied. "George kept his money in a biscuit tin, under the settee in the studio. I told him once that he ought to keep it locked up, but he only laughed at me. He said that no one in Port Bosun would dream of helping himself to it."

"Did you know, before Mr. Hawken's death, how much money he had in the biscuit tin?" Arnold asked.

"I had no idea," Paul replied. "It wasn't until next day, when I opened the tin, that I found twenty-six pounds odd in it."

"And you told us that Mr. Hawken never locked the door when he went out," said Arnold. "Now I put this suggestion to you, Mr. Clapdale. Is it not possible that on the day of Mr. Hawken's death the tin contained more than twenty-six pounds, and that the balance had been taken by some person not resident in Port Bosun?"

"The idea had not occurred to me," Paul replied. "Who do you suspect of having taken the money?"

"Some person who knew that Mr. Hawken kept his money in a tin, and where that tin was to be found," said Arnold. "Was Mr. Hawken in the habit of entertaining visitors in the studio?"

Paul shook his head. "Never, so far as I am aware. If George had visitors, which wasn't very often, he used to take them into the front room. I was the exception. If George was at work when I called he would take me into the studio and go on painting while we talked. I don't suppose that many other people in Port Bosun went into the studio while George was alive."

"Has Barry Benson ever stayed in this cottage?" Arnold asked.

"He has stayed here with his uncle sometimes when he was out of a job," Paul replied. "And that was fairly often. I strongly suspect that on those occasions George gave Barry money, though he never told me that he had."

"Then he was more generous than his brother," said Arnold. "I can tell you this, Mr. Clapdale. On the Sunday before Mr. George Hawken's death, Barry went to Moat Barn to try to get some money from Sir Matthew, who refused to see him."

"I'm not surprised to hear that," Paul replied. "George told me that his brother disapproved of Barry, whom he described as a vagabond. Barry can't have had great hopes of persuading Sir Matthew to give him any money. Before I forget it, Mr. Arnold. Would you be good enough to give me Sir Matthew's full address?"

Arnold gave it to him, and Paul wrote it down in a notebook which he habitually carried.

"Thank you very much, Mr. Arnold," he said. "I can now tell the removal people where to send the pictures. I shall of course write to Sir Matthew, telling him to expect them."

"Talking of the pictures," said Arnold. "You told us, I think, that Mr. Hawken occasionally sold one of them. How did he set about it?"

"The true answer to that is that he didn't set about it," Paul replied. "He just waited for the buyer to come along. You see there are quite a lot of artists in this part of the country, and the dealers come along at intervals to look at their work. Sometimes, but not very often, they used to call on George. A few weeks ago one of them did actually call."

"Did he buy any of Mr. Hawken's pictures?" Arnold asked.

"He did indeed," Paul replied. "I happened to drop in on the day that the dealer was here. George introduced me to him, and his name, if I remember right, was Green. He was a curious sombre sort of chap, dressed all in black. I didn't stop, because I saw that George was talking business with him. But next day George told me that he had brought off one of the best deals of his life. The dealer had bought two of his pictures, and paid him a hundred and twenty pounds for them."

"Can you tell me when this was?" Arnold asked.

"I can't tell you the exact date," Paul replied. "But it was about the middle of May. The dealer paid George the money in notes."

"Which I suppose, Mr. Hawken put in the biscuit tin?" Arnold asked.

"Naturally," Paul replied. "As I have told you, that was where he always kept his money."

"Mr. Hawken was killed on June the fourteenth," said Arnold. "Roughly a month after he received the money from the dealer. Yet, after his death, you found only twenty-six pounds in the tin. Is Mr. Hawken likely to have spent just under a hundred pounds in four weeks?"

"Good heavens, Mr. Arnold!" Paul exclaimed. "I've never looked on it that way before. No, it's most unlikely that George spent all that money on himself. I don't suppose that his expenses, including canvas, paint and that sort of thing were more than three or four pounds a week. But, of course, he may have given some of the money away."

"Who is he likely to have given it to?" Arnold asked.

Paul shook his head. "That I cannot say. George wouldn't have told me. But he was a most generous soul. If any of the fishermen had been in trouble, George would have been the first to help him."

"Well, perhaps that's where the money went," said Arnold. "Might we see the place where the tin box is kept?"

"By all means," Paul replied. "Come with me, and I'll show you." He led them out of the kitchen, through the front room and so into the studio. Against one wall stood an old-fashioned and much worn settee, which had a strip of some material hanging from the seat almost to the floor. Paul raised this, to expose a square biscuit tin.

He drew it out and removed the lid. Inside were a number of pieces of paper. "Receipts for rates," Paul explained. "If he had any other receipts, George doesn't seem to have kept them. I don't suppose he had many, because he always used to pay in cash for everything he bought."

"Is it possible that Mr. Hawken kept money in any other place?" Arnold asked.

"I'm sure he didn't," Paul replied. "As George's executor I felt it to be my duty to search the cottage thoroughly. I found no money or papers of any kind."

"Thank you, Mr. Clapdale," said Arnold. "We have nothing more to do here. Can we give you a lift home?"

Paul accepted the offer, and they went out, Paul locking the cottage door behind them and putting the key in his pocket. Egford drove to Merrymount and deposited Paul at his gate. Then he turned the car and drove back into the village.

"I want a word with Docking," he said.

They found Docking in his shirt-sleeves, trimming the hedge which separated his house from the village street. He sprang to attention as the car drew up.

"I beg your pardon, sir," he said apologetically. "I didn't know you were coming, or I'd have been properly dressed."

"That's all right, Constable," Egford replied. "Now, can you tell me this? Has anyone in the village been in financial difficulties during the past few weeks?"

"Not that I've heard, sir," said Docking, "and if anyone had been short of money it would have come to my ears for sure. That sort of thing gets about in no time in a little place like this."

"Well, nose round and see if you can find out anything. And if you do, let me know."

Arnold and Egford drove back to Thramsbury Police Station and repaired to the superintendent's room.

"The question is, who knew where that biscuit tin was kept," said Arnold. "No casual visitor to the studio would have seen it. Under the settee wasn't a bad place for the money. Better than under the mattress or in the cracked teapot on the mantelpiece. In any case, we are told that Mr. Hawken didn't often entertain visitors in the studio."

"On the other hand, anyone who had stayed in the house would probably have learnt where the tin was. Barry had stayed with his uncle who, no doubt, had given him money on those occasions. Barry would have seen his uncle take out the tin and put it back again."

"You think that Barry took money from the tin on the day of his uncle's death?" Egford asked.

"I feel pretty sure of it," Arnold replied. "Either before or after he pushed his uncle over the edge. More likely after. He had a little while to wait for the bus back to Thramsbury, and he wouldn't have cared to hang about the village where he might be recognised. So he hid up in Cliff Cottage. There was no difficulty about getting in, since the door was not locked.

"He knew where the biscuit tin was kept, and he looked into it. He found a lot of money in it, far more than he could have expected. Here was a way of getting over his financial difficulties, at least temporarily. His uncle would have no further use for money, so Barry helped himself to something like a hundred pounds."

"Why didn't he take the lot while he was about it?" Egford asked.

"Because he didn't want the theft to be discovered," Arnold replied. "He knew that, his uncle being dead, the tin would be opened. If it were found empty, suspicion would be aroused. Mr. Hawken must have had at least a few pounds by him at the time of his death. The only explanation could be that the tin had been robbed."

"So that when Barry went off, he had a considerable sum of money in his possession," said Egford. "With that, he might have gone almost anywhere. Do you still believe that he went to London?"

"I'm beginning to doubt it," Arnold replied. "If he went to London, we ought to have had some word of him by now. As you say, he might have gone anywhere in this country. He might even have gone abroad, by going on one of those no passport trips and not returning. Well, I've found out what I wanted to know, and there's nothing else I can do here now. If anything crops up, you've only got to give me a ring, and I'll come down again."

Chapter V

Shepherd Green cricket week opened on 10th July in glorious weather. Merrion and Mavis had arrived at the vicarage on the previous evening, and their host, who was a bachelor, had invited Mrs. Aintree to dinner to keep Mavis company. After dinner, the ladies had retired to the drawing-room, while the men remained to drink a glass of port together. Luke Dedham, whose knowledge of wine was extensive, prided himself upon his port.

As soon as they were alone together, Luke broached the subject of the next day's match.

"We always open the week with a local Derby," he said. "We're playing the next village, Yarndown, and naturally we're all out to beat them. But we're suffering under a great misfortune. Our crack batsman sprained his wrist last week while he was felling a tree, and he says he won't be able to hold a bat. I'm counting on you to take his place."

Merrion laughed. "As I've told you before, my cricketing days are over. If I were to consent to take your man's place, you'd find me a broken reed. I should only make an exhibition of myself."

"You will," said Luke. "But not in the sense you mean. You will exhibit to our local worthies what scientific batsmanship can be. Come on, now, Desmond. You wouldn't have the heart to let down Shepherd Green, would you?"

"I don't feel under any obligation to Shepherd Green," Merrion replied. "But, as your guest, I am under an obligation to you, and I would like to be able to meet it. But how can I possibly play? I've got no proper kit with me. You don't expect me to bat in a lounge suit, do you?"

"That's easily got over," said Luke. "I've got plenty of shirts and white trousers. We're much of a size, and my things will fit you well enough. I can even lend you a blazer in the Shepherd Green colours. So that's settled."

"Very well then," Merrion replied. "If I must play, I must, I suppose. But if I'm bowled out first ball, you'll only have yourself to blame. I haven't held a bat for years.'

"I'll chance it," said Luke. "I'll rig you out in the morning. By the way, a friend of yours was at Moat Barn not long ago. I happened to call when he was there and we had a short chat, mainly about cricket."

"What was Arnold doing at Moat Barn?" Merrion asked.

Luke shook his head. "I don't know. He and Francine Paris had a conversation, but neither of them told me what it was about."

"I dare say it was in connection with the death of Sir Matthew's brother," said Merrion. "You heard about that, I suppose?"

"Yes, Sir Matthew told me," Luke replied. "I go to see him at least once a week. I seem to be one of the few people he cares to talk to. He told me that his nephew, Hubert Benson, had brought him the news. Sir Matthew was greatly distressed, and it took him some time to get over the shock. It seems that Mr. George Hawken, who was also an artist, left his brother his pictures. They arrived at Moat Barn a week or two ago, and Sir Matthew let me see them."

"What opinion of them did you form?" Merrion asked.

"I don't profess to be an art critic," Luke replied. "The pictures didn't make a great impression on me. In most cases I found it difficult to understand what the artist had been driving at. But Sir Matthew, who is a first-class judge of art, told me that they were superlative work. Far better than anything he had produced himself. It was due to public ignorance that while his own pictures had sold readily, his brother's hadn't."

"What is Sir Matthew going to do with them?" Merrion asked.

"He's going to hang them," Luke replied. "It appears that there isn't enough room for them in that great studio of his. So he means to have some of his own pictures moved up into the gallery, to make room for his brother's. I should very much like you to see the interior of Moat Barn. But Sir Matthew is very difficult about meeting strangers."

Meanwhile Mavis and Mrs. Aintree were chatting in the drawing-room. Amabel Aintree had once been a famous beauty, and was now married to John Aintree, who was in business in the City. They lived at Shepherd Manor, a Jacobean house about half a mile from the vicarage. John's business constantly took him about the country, and he was at present in Manchester.

Amabel Aintree was one of those people who call everyone by their Christian names on first acquaintance.

"It is so nice to meet you again, Mavis," she was saying. "It seems ages since you were here last. It was sweet of Luke to invite me here this evening. But then that's like him, always so thoughtful. Now that you're going to be here for a whole week, I shall make it my business to introduce you to some of my friends. I wish I could take you to see Sir Matthew, but he's almost inaccessible, even to me. I do think he might show some friendliness towards a woman whose portrait he painted when she was a girl."Mavis did not tell her that she too had been painted by Sir Matthew.

"It's all the fault of that dressed up hussy!" Amabel went on. "I'm sure that Sir Matthew would like to see me, but she won't let him. She wants to keep him to herself. I think it's disgraceful. I've spoken to Luke about it more than once. I told him that it was his duty to reprove the immorality of his parishioners. All he said was that there was nothing immoral about Francine Paris. Would you believe it? But there, men always shut their eyes to what they don't want to see."

Village cricket is subject to a law of necessity. Since most of the players are in regular employment, they cannot devote the whole day to the game. A match usually begins at half-past two in the afternoon, and ends that same evening. Further, play is usually restricted to Saturdays. Only on exceptional occasions, such as Shepherd Green cricket week, can arrangements be made for matches on other weekdays.

So, after lunch on Monday, Merrion, in borrowed plumes, accompanied Luke from the vicarage to the field. Their way was by the road leading to Moat Barn. But before they reached the mound on which the house stood, they turned off along a path which crossed several cuts by means of plank bridges. This brought them to a field among the marshes, on which was a small wooden pavilion. From the field they could see the back of Moat Barn, and the terrace which partly surrounded it.

"I expect you'll see Sir Matthew sitting up there before long," said Luke. "If the weather is fine and sunny, as it is to-day, he always comes out to watch. With his binoculars he has an excellent view. But you won't see him yet, because he always sleeps for an hour or so after his lunch. The doctor insists upon that."

The players began to arrive, on foot and on bicycles. When both sides were assembled, Luke and the Yarndown captain tossed up. Luke won the toss, and elected to bat first. Spectators drifted on to the field, among them Mavis and Amabel, and took their seats on a row of benches beside the pavilion. The match started, and before it had proceeded for many minutes, Sir Matthew appeared on the terrace, wheeled there by Francine. Albert Oakley was one of the Shepherd Green players. Sir Matthew always allowed him the afternoon off on these occasions. He was Shepherd Green's star bowler.

Merrion scored twenty-three before he was caught in the slips. It was the highest score of the day. Shepherd Green's last wicket fell with a total of eighty-one, and Yarndown went in to bat. They started badly, Albert Oakley taking two wickets in his first over. After that they rallied, and were all out for sixty-seven. Both teams adjourned to the Greyhound, the village inn, for tea.

Next day, Shepherd Green were not so lucky, being beaten by Brockbridge by the narrow margin of three runs. Merrion again put up a most creditable performance. And on Wednesday the weather changed. By dawn it was raining heavily, and at breakfast Luke was pessimistic.

"It doesn't look as if there would be any play to-day," he said. "Unless it clears up within the next hour or so we shall have to abandon our fixture with Mendlehurst. And that's not the worst of it. If it goes on like this the rest of the week will be ruined."

"Oh, surely not!" Mavis exclaimed. "It's sure to stop raining to-morrow."

"That won't help us," Luke replied. "If it doesn't stop raining until to-morrow, the pitch will be flooded. It lies so low that it always floods after twenty-four hours' steady rain, though that doesn't often happen at this time of year. In winter it's more often under water than not. The pavilion is a sectional affair, and at the end of the season we dismantle it and move it to higher ground. Sir Matthew lets us put it into one of his out-houses until the start of the next season."

It continued to rain all the morning. After lunch Luke and Merrion, wearing mackintoshes, set out for the field to inspect its condition. Just before they turned off the road, they were met by Albert Oakley, riding fast on his bicycle. Seeing Luke, he slowed down.

"Sir Matthew's been taken bad, sir," he said. "I'm on my way to fetch the doctor."

Then, increasing his pace again, he rode on.

"I hope it's nothing serious," said Luke, as he and Merrion went on their way. "Considering his age, Sir Matthew enjoys remarkably good health. The credit is largely due to Francine, who looks after him most devotedly. One can't ring up to inquire, because there is no telephone at Moat Barn. But I'll ring up Dick Kent later on, and hear what his report is."

As they crossed the bridges on the way to the field, Merrion noticed that the water in the cuts was much higher than it had been on the previous day. When they reached the field they found that it was not actually under water, but as they walked across it water oozed from under their shoes.

"Not so bad as it might have been," Luke remarked. "Fortunately, the water in the marshes falls as quickly as it rises. If the rain stops by the evening, the pitch may be fit to play on to-morrow."

"It's not raining nearly so hard as it was," Merrion replied. "And I fancy the wind has gone round a bit. With any luck the weather should clear, and play will be possible to-morrow."

"I sincerely hope it will," said Luke. "Everyone in the village looks forward to the cricket week, and it would be a thousand pities if they were disappointed."

They turned back, and as they neared the road, they saw the doctor's car driving along it towards Moat Barn.

"That's good," said Luke. "Dick has wasted no time. He never does when he's called to see a patient. We shall have to wait till he gets home before we ask him for his news."

By the time they got back to the vicarage, Merrion's prediction was fulfilled, and the rain had stopped.

"I should feel jubilant if I wasn't so anxious about Sir Matthew," said Luke. "I shan't rest until I've heard what Dick has to say about him. The garden is too wet to be fit to sit in. Shall we join Mavis?"

"I don't expect she's in," Merrion replied. "She told me that Mrs. Aintree was coming in her car to fetch her this afternoon."

"Then let's go into my study and talk," said Luke. "There are lots of things I wanted to say to you. But my head has been full of nothing but cricket since you've been here."

The two old friends found plenty to talk about, since they had many acquaintances and interests in common. Their conversation was interrupted by the opening of the study door, and the voice of Mrs. Welback, Luke's housekeeper.

"Dr. Kent to see you, sir."

Richard Kent came in looking very grave. There was no need of an introduction to Merrion, since the two had already met on the cricket field.

"I've some very bad news for you, Luke," said the doctor. "An hour ago I was summoned to Moat Barn. When I got there, I found Sir Matthew dead. I've just come from there, and I want your advice, Luke."

Merrion rose to his feet. "I'll take a turn or two round the garden while you two have your chat," he said.

"Please don't go, Mr. Merrion," Dick replied. "I may need your advice as well. Luke has told me that you have a friend at Scotland Yard. In fact I saw him at Moat Barn not so long ago."

Merrion resumed his seat, and Dick went on. "What I am going to say is entirely between ourselves, of course. It's amazing that Sir Matthew should have died so suddenly. He was perfectly fit when I last saw him two or three days ago, and Francine tells me that he was well enough this morning to entertain a visitor. I don't like the look of it at all."

"What did Sir Matthew die of?" Luke asked.

"That's just it," Dick replied. "The appearances are those of acute poisoning. Mind you, that is only my own opinion, and I don't profess to be a toxicologist. I cannot issue a certificate, because only a post-mortem can determine the cause of death. On the other hand, I don't want to cause a lot of fuss and bother. What am I to do, Luke?"

"This is a very serious matter," said Luke. "Do you imagine that Sir Matthew was poisoned deliberately?"

"Let me repeat that I cannot be certain that the cause of his death was poisoning," Dick replied. "If it was, how could Sir Matthew have taken poison accidentally? Nobody who knew him as we did could imagine for a moment that he poisoned himself. And I refuse to believe that either Francine or Albert Oakley poisoned him."

"I fully agree with you," said Luke. "If you feel unable to issue a certificate, that will mean an inquest, I suppose. What do you think Dick ought to do, Desmond? Inform the police?"

"I hardly think that that is necessary at this stage," Merrion replied. "Not until it has been confirmed that the cause of death was poisoning. If I were in the doctor's place, I should inform the coroner immediately. I should say that I was unable to determine the cause of death, but I should not mention my suspicions. The coroner will no doubt ask the county pathologist to perform a post-mortem. If that establishes the fact that Sir Matthew's death was due to poisoning, then the police will be called upon."

"That is most excellent advice, Mr. Merrion!" Dick exclaimed. "I shall certainly act upon it. I'll go home now and ring up the coroner."

Luke showed him to the door and returned.

"This is most distressing," he said as he sat down. "The death of Sir Matthew is bad enough, but this horrible suggestion of poisoning is far worse. I don't doubt that Dick is right about that. Diagnosis has always been his strong point. What do you make of it all, Desmond?"

"The first thing that strikes me is this," Merrion replied. "It seems remarkable that Sir Matthew should have died suddenly and mysteriously so soon after his brother's fatal accident. If indeed it was an accident."

"What do you mean?" Luke exclaimed. "Have you any reason to suspect that it was not an accident?"

"The jury returned an open verdict," Merrion replied. "It is possible that Mr. George Hawken was the victim of foul play. Is it not equally possible that Sir Matthew's sudden death was also due to foul play?"

"I refuse to believe it possible," said Luke firmly. "It is inconceivable that either Francine or Albert Oakley should have poisoned Sir Matthew. And no one else could have had the opportunity."

The door opened, and Mrs. Welback again appeared. "Miss Paris is here, sir," she said. "She asked me if she could see you alone."

"This time I really will leave you to it," said Merrion. The study had a french window overlooking the lawn. This stood open, and he went out by it. At the farther side of the lawn was a gravelled path, and he strolled up and down this, considering the doctor's story. If his suspicion of poisoning turned out to be correct, had Sir Matthew been murdered? And if so by whom?

By one of the members of his household, seemed to be the obvious answer. Luke was convinced that neither of them would have done such a thing, but his conviction was not evidence. Merrion knew so little of either of them that he did not feel competent to form an opinion of his own.

Failing murder, what then? In these days of chemical pest destroyers, poisons, some of them extremely toxic, were to be found in nearly every garden. Accident with one of these was a possibility, though it was difficult to understand how such an accident could have happened.

Both Luke and the doctor were sure that Sir Matthew had not committed suicide. In any case, it was hard to explain how a man whose only means of locomotion was a wheeled chair could have secured the poison and swallowed it without the knowledge of his attendants.

Merrion had come to the conclusion that murder was the most likely explanation of Sir Matthew's death when Luke appeared at the study window.

"Come along, Desmond," he called. "Miss Paris has gone, and tea is ready."

Merrion crossed the lawn, and he and Luke entered the house together. Mrs. Welback had laid tea in the drawing-room.

"Francine is terribly upset," said Luke as he filled the two cups. "I did my best to comfort her, and told her that she couldn't have expected Sir Matthew to live much longer. He was eighty-six, you know. I asked Francine to stay to tea, but she said she would rather not do that, as she felt she must get back to Moat Barn. She told me that she had been to the post office to send telegrams. One to Hubert Benson, and another to Mr. Bridgwater, Sir Matthew's solicitor, who has just come back from a cruise. She would have sent one to Barry Benson, but she didn't know where he was."

"Dr. Kent had not told Miss Paris what he suspected,"

Merrion remarked. "Has she formed any suspicions herself?"

"I don't think so," Luke replied. "If she has, she didn't mention them. She seems too dazed by the suddenness of it to speculate upon the cause of death."

Dick followed Merrion's advice. He communicated with the coroner, informing him of Sir Matthew's death, the cause of which he was unable to determine. The coroner replied that he would arrange for the county pathologist to examine the body. Later that afternoon the pathologist rang up Dick. He had been requested by the coroner to examine the body of Sir Matthew Hawken. He proposed to do so at eleven o'clock next morning. He would drive to Dr. Kent's house, and would ask him to guide him to the house in which the body lay.

Dick agreed to this. On Thursday morning the pathologist arrived punctually. Dick took the seat beside him, and showed him the way to Moat Barn. On their arrival they found the drawbridge lowered, and they walked up the path to the door. Dick knocked on it, and it was opened by Albert Oakley.

"Have you come to see Miss Paris, sir?" he asked Dick. "I'm sorry that she's out. She has gone to the vicarage to see Mr. Dedham."

"I'm not sorry for that," Dick replied. "My friend and I have come to examine Sir Matthew's body. I'd like you to keep guard outside the door, and see that no one comes in to interrupt us. Even Miss Paris, if she comes back while we are here."

"Very good, sir," Albert replied. He went out, and the pathologist opened the case which he had brought with him. The body was lying partly clothed in the four-poster bed. Having made his preparations the pathologist approached it.

"Not a very suitable place for a post-mortem," he said. "But we shall have to make do as best we can."

With Dick's assistance he carried out a full examination.

"No doubt about the cause of death," he said when he had finished. "All the appearances indicate that the dead man swallowed some poisonous substance. One of the cyanides, I think, but I cannot be sure of that until I have analysed the contents of the stomach. What do you know about this, Kent?"

"How he came to swallow poison passes my comprehension," Dick replied. "I feel quite sure that it was not administered by either of his attendants. When I saw the body yesterday I suspected poisoning. But as I could not be certain of that, I did not tell the coroner so."

"I shall make it my business to do that," said the pathologist. "And not only the coroner, but the police as well. Any case of poisoning must be a matter for investigation. The Chief Constable is a personal friend of mine, and I shall go straight to him."He and Dick left Moat Barn and returned to the car. The pathologist dropped Dick at his house, then drove on to Dersham, the county town, fifteen miles from Shepherd Green. He called first on the coroner, and had a conversation with him. At its conclusion, the coroner said that he would arrange to hold an inquest, sitting with a jury, at Shepherd Green at two-thirty the following afternoon.

The pathologist then visited his friend the Chief Constable at police headquarters, and told him his story.

"It looks to me like an ugly business," he went on. "A man confined to an invalid-chair isn't likely to have swallowed poison by accident. Dr. Kent assures me that Sir Matthew, who had been his patient for years, would never have committed suicide. And there's only one alternative."

"I shall call in the Yard," the chief replied. "In a case like this my people won't feel that their backs have been rubbed up the wrong way, in fact, they'll probably feel relieved that the responsibility has been taken from their shoulders. Sir Matthew's name was well known, and his death is bound to become front page news, especially if the verdict is murder."

"I think you're wise," said the pathologist. "I'll get my analysis done this afternoon. It will be a very simple one, if the poison was what I think it was. Then I shall be in a position to give definite evidence at the inquest."

Chapter VI

When the Assistant Commissioner received the message from Dersham, it was natural that he should detail Arnold for the job. Arnold had been to Moat Barn already, and was therefore to some extent familiar with the conditions there. He travelled by train to Dersham that afternoon, and was met by Inspector Filland of the local constabulary.

Filland drove Arnold to police headquarters and introduced him to the Chief Constable.

"I'm very glad to meet you, Mr. Arnold," said the chief. "I must warn you that this is a case in which you'll have to start at the beginning. Sir Matthew Hawken died suddenly yesterday, and the pathologist reports that his death was due to poisoning. We have no evidence as to how the poison was administered. You have heard of Sir Matthew, no doubt?" "I have, sir," Arnold replied. "And, though I did not meet him, I was at Moat Barn some weeks ago, inquiring about one of his nephews."

"Excellent!" the chief exclaimed. "Then you'll know your way about. Filland will drive you there, and you can ask such questions as you think fit. Let me know what you learn."

Filland drove Arnold to Moat Barn. The drawbridge was lowered, and they walked up the path to the house. Francine opened the door at their knock.

"Why, Mr. Arnold!" she exclaimed. "So you've come here again? If it's about Barry Benson, I can't tell you anything. There has been no word from him since you were last here."

"It isn't about Mr. Benson this time, Miss Paris," Arnold replied. "Inspector Filland and I have come to obtain particulars of the death of Sir Matthew Hawken. Will you tell us what you know about it?"

"Of course I will," said Francine. "But if we don't want to be interrupted, you had better come into my room. Hubert Benson and Mr. Bridgwater are here."

She led them across the studio to a door at the farther side. She opened this and showed them into a large room, furnished as a bed-sitting-room. "Do sit down, and tell me exactly what you want to know."

"Who was the first person to find that Sir Matthew was dead?" Arnold asked.

"I was," she replied. "I had been into the village in. the morning, to order some things to be sent here from the shops. There is no telephone here, so either Albert Oakley or I have to go into the village to give the orders. I came back just in time to find a visitor leaving.

Albert told me that he had been sitting with Sir Matthew in the studio.

"A few minutes later lunch was ready, and Sir Matthew and I had it in the studio, as it was raining. When the weather was fine we usually had lunch on the terrace. Albert had cooked the lunch and brought it to us. Sir Matthew was perfectly well and asked me whom I had met in the village. He always liked hearing about people, though he didn't always want to see them. He also said that it was a pity it was so wet, as it would make cricket impossible that afternoon. He didn't mention the visitor, so I thought it better not to ask any questions about him."

The mention of cricket recalled to Arnold's memory that the parson had told him that he had invited the Merrions to stay with him for the local cricket week. If Merrion was at the vicarage now, it would be a great stroke of luck. He put the thought aside for the moment and continued his interrogation.

"Sir Matthew seemed perfectly well at lunch, Miss Paris?"

"Perfectly," Francine replied. "And he had a very good appetite. When we had finished lunch, I wheeled him in here and gave him his tablet. Sir Matthew had complained of slight indigestion last winter, and Dr. Kent had prescribed some tablets for him. He had been taking one after each meal ever since. "Sir Matthew always went to bed for an hour or so after his lunch. I helped him from his chair into the bed, and saw that he was comfortably settled. Then, as I always did, I came into this room, leaving the door open, so that I should hear if Sir Matthew called, as he used to when he awoke and wanted help to get up.

"There was no call, and after an hour I went into the studio to see if Sir Matthew was awake. He seemed to be fast asleep, so I did not attempt to disturb him. I sat down in the studio, expecting every minute that Sir Matthew would wake. I waited perhaps twenty minutes, then went to the bed again. Sir Matthew was perfectly motionless, and his face was a pallor which I had never seen before. I tried to rouse him, but failed. I knew that he must be ill, and I sent Albert for Dr. Kent. While I was waiting, I watched Sir Matthew for any sign of returning consciousness, but there was none. When Dr. Kent came he examined Sir Matthew, and told me that he was dead, and had been for at least an hour, possibly longer."

"Then Sir Matthew must have died very shortly after eating his lunch," said Arnold. "Did he eat anything which you did not?"

Francine shook her head. "No, all three of us, Sir Matthew, Albert and myself, all had the same lunch. Roast shoulder of lamb, with peas and new potatoes from the garden. After that, gooseberry-pie and cheese and biscuits. Sir Matthew liked his principal meal in the middle of the day, and a light supper. The only thing he had that Albert and I didn't was his digestive tablet."

"Where were the tablets kept?" Arnold asked.

"On the table by the bedside in the studio," Francine replied. "There were only about a dozen tablets left in the box, and I was going to ask Dr. Kent to let Sir Matthew have some more."

"About the visitor who came to see Sir Matthew yesterday morning," said Arnold. "What can you tell me about him?"

"Very little," Francine replied. "I only saw him for a moment. He was leaving the house as I came in. He was a short man, wearing a black raincoat and a black hat. As I came back from the village I saw that the drawbridge was down, and a car standing in the road with a chauffeur sitting in it."

"Was Sir Matthew expecting this visitor?" Arnold asked.

"I didn't know that he was," Francine replied. "But he must have been, or it is most unlikely that he would have seen him. He rarely or never saw strangers except by appointment. Albert told me that the visitor sat in the studio with Sir Matthew for about a quarter of an hour. It ended by Sir Matthew telling the visitor to clear out and not come here again."

"Could we see Albert Oakley?" Arnold asked.

"Certainly," Francine replied. "Shall I bring him here, or would you rather see him in the kitchen?"

"In the kitchen, I think," said Arnold. She led them from the room and crossed the studio to a door under the gallery. She opened this, to disclose a well-fitted kitchen. Albert was standing by the sink, peeling potatoes.

"These gentlemen wish to speak to you, Albert," said Francine.

She went back to the studio as Albert turned.

"We've met before, Oakley," said Arnold. "You remember letting me in a few weeks ago? And this is Inspector Filland from Dersham. Miss Paris tells us that Sir Matthew had a visitor yesterday morning. Do you know who he was?"

"No, I don't, sir," Albert replied. "This was the way of it. Miss Paris had gone out, and I had raised the drawbridge after her. Sir Matthew always liked it kept raised, so that people couldn't get up to the house. I was on the lookout for Miss Paris to come back, so that I could lower the bridge for her, when I saw a car drive up. I went along to see who it was, just as I did when you came here, sir. The car was driven by a chauffeur, and sitting beside him was a gentleman dressed all in black, just like an undertaker's man. I asked the gentleman if he had an appointment with Sir Matthew, and he said he had. He showed me one of Sir Matthew's cards and written on it in Sir Matthew's handwriting was 'Wednesday 12th July, morning'."

"Was it usual for Sir Matthew to send a card to people with whom he wished to make an appointment?" Arnold asked.

"I think he must have, sir," Albert replied. "It wasn't the first time that I had been shown a card with his writing on it. As I took the gentleman up the path I asked him his name, but he said it didn't matter, because Sir Matthew would know him when he saw him. So I showed the gentleman into the studio, where Sir Matthew was. Then I went up to the gallery, where my quarters are. I sleep up there, so that there was no door between me and Sir Matthew when he went to bed. I could hear Sir Matthew when he called in the night, as he sometimes did. If he was wakeful, he liked me to make him a glass of hot milk."

"Could you hear the conversation between Sir Matthew and his visitor?" Arnold asked.

"Not clearly, sir," Albert replied. "I only caught a word here and there, and I gathered it was about pictures. And then, after a while Sir Matthew got angry and raised his voice. I heard him tell the gentleman that he wouldn't consider anything of the kind. If that was what he had come for, he had forced an interview under false pretences. He was to clear out, and never to come here again. Sir Matthew, who was sitting in his chair, wheeled himself into Miss Paris's room and slammed the door behind him."

"Could Sir Matthew get out of his chair without assistance?" Arnold asked.

"He could if he had to, sir," Albert replied, "and he could walk a few steps by himself. As far as the lavatory, for instance. I came down from the gallery to show the visitor out. He didn't seem in the least upset by what Sir Matthew had said to him. He was standing in the studio, looking at the pictures, which were left on the walls. I had taken some of them down, on Sir Matthew's orders. It was to make room for Mr. George Hawken's pictures, which are still in cases in the storeroom.

"As I went out with the gentleman, Miss Paris came in. She looked surprised to find that someone was here. I took the gentleman down to his car, and when he had got into it, I pulled up the drawbridge. After what Sir Matthew had said, I didn't want him to try to come back again. Then I came back to the kitchen to get lunch ready."

"How long have you been in Sir Matthew's service?" Arnold asked.

"Longer than you might think, sir," Albert replied. "It's a matter of forty years now. This is how it came about. In the First War I was a young soldier, serving at a base in France. Mr. Matthew Hawken, as he was then, wasn't a regular soldier, but he was sent out as a war artist, and I was told off to be his batman. When the war was over, and I was demobbed, Mr. Hawken asked me to come to him as his cook and valet. I was very glad to do that, and I've been with him ever since."

"And what will you do now?" Arnold asked.

Albert shrugged his shoulders. "That I can't say, sir. It won't be easy for me to find another job at my age. I shall just have to wait and see what happens."

"When lunch was ready yesterday, what did you do?" Arnold asked.

"I'd got the table laid in the studio, sir," Albert replied. "Usually, when it's fine, Sir Matthew and Miss Paris had their lunch on the terrace, but it was no weather for that yesterday. I carved two helpings of the joint in here, and put some potatoes and peas on the plates. Then I took them into the studio. When Sir Matthew and Miss Paris had finished I cleared away their plates and brought them two helpings of gooseberry-pie."

"Did Sir Matthew and Miss Paris have anything to drink with their lunch?" Arnold asked.

"Yes, sir," Albert replied. "They each of them had a glass or two of hock. Sir Matthew always drank white wine in warm weather."

"Did you see Sir Matthew take his tablet after lunch?" Arnold asked.

"Yes, sir," Albert replied. "I was in the studio, clearing up. I saw Miss Paris take a tablet from the box and give it to Sir Matthew. He swallowed it and washed it down with a sip of wine. Then I came in here and had my own lunch, the same as the others, except that I didn't drink wine, though I could have if I'd wanted to. I don't care much for it, so I had a bottle of beer instead."

"Were there any visitors here yesterday besides the man in black?" Arnold asked.

"Not in the morning, sir," Albert replied. "Charlie Potter came along, but you wouldn't call him a visitor. He didn't stop very long, because it was too wet for him to do anything. He told me he might come back in the afternoon, but so far as I know he never did."

"Who is Charlie Potter?" Arnold asked.

"He's the gardener, sir," Albert replied. "He doesn't come here regular, but puts in a few hours when he thinks he will. But when he does come, his work is first class, as he's been a gardener all his life. He was head gardener for Mr. Aintree at the manor before he drew his old-age pension. Then he gave up the job."

"Have you seen him since yesterday?" Arnold asked.

"He was here this morning," Albert replied. "He had some cock and bull story about his smock and apron having been stolen. He seemed to think that I must have taken them. And when I had made him understand that Sir Matthew was dead, he told me that he wouldn't be coming here any longer. That wouldn't be any loss to him, because there were plenty of folk in the village always at him to do a few hours' work for them."

"Where does this man Potter live?" Arnold asked.

"It's the first house on the left as you go from here towards the village, sir," Albert replied. "But you're more likely to find him at the Greyhound in opening hours. He's a proper tippler, is Charlie."

"I dare say I shall make his acquaintance," said Arnold. "Miss Paris told us that Mr. Bridgwater and Mr. Benson were here. Did they arrive together?"

Albert shook his head. "No, sir. Mr. Bridgwater came here this morning. He took a taxi from Dersham Station. Mr. Hubert came only an hour or so before you did, sir. He drove down from London in his own car."

"What became of the car?" Arnold asked. "I didn't see it when we drove up just now."

"You wouldn't, sir," Albert replied. "Mr. Hubert drove it around the side of the mount, off the road. There's an open space there where a car can be parked."

"I see," said Arnold. "Now look here, Oakley. I want to talk to Mr. Bridgwater privately, somewhere we shan't be interrupted. Could you do something about that?"

Albert considered this for a few moments. "Well, I don't know, sir," he replied apologetically. "This ain't like an ordinary house. There are no sitting-rooms, so to say. But if you wouldn't mind seeing Mr. Bridgwater in the pantry, no one will come in there."

Arnold smiled. "I've no objection to the pantry, and I dare say Mr. Bridgwater won't have any either. Show me the way."

The pantry adjoined the kitchen separated from it by a door. Albert opened this then, taking three chairs from the kitchen, carried them through. Arnold and Filland followed him, to find themselves in a room lined with loaded shelves.

"This will do very well," he said, taking a card from his pocket. "Will you show this to Mr. Bridgwater, and tell him that I should like to speak to him? And, if he agrees, bring him here."

"Mr. Bridgwater is on the terrace with Mr. Hubert, sir," Albert replied. "I'll go and find him." He went out, to return shortly with an elderly man with a slightly bewildered expression.

"Well, here I am," he said. "I don't understand the police

being in the house. What's it all about?"

"Will you sit down, Mr. Bridgwater?" Arnold replied. "Inspector Filland and I are here to inquire into the death of Sir Matthew Hawken."

Bridgwater took the chair which Arnold offered him. "That sounds rather ominous," he said. "Am I to infer that there is reason to suspect that Matthew's death was not due to natural causes?"

"That will become apparent at the inquest tomorrow," Arnold replied. "I am given to understand that in the past you have acted for Sir Matthew."

"That is correct," Bridgwater replied. "I have acted for him since my father's death, many years ago. But before I tell you anything else, I had better make my position clear. Early in May I went on an extensive cruise, and I only returned to my office last Monday. I had given orders that no correspondence was to be forwarded to me while I was away. When I am on holiday I like to put business affairs entirely out of my mind."

"As you may suppose, I found a mass of correspondence awaiting my attention. Among it was a letter from Matthew, written about a week ago. The letter was to the effect that since George had been killed, Matthew would have to make a fresh will. Would I come and see him at my convenience? This was the first news I had had of George's death. I should have come here within the next few days, but yesterday I had a telegram from Miss Paris, telling me that Matthew was dead. I therefore came here this morning. I have had the opportunity of a long conversation with Miss Paris, who told me the facts as she knew them."

"You won't mind if I ask you a few questions, Mr. Bridgwater?" said Arnold. "To begin with, can you tell us who gains to any extent by the death of Sir Matthew?"

"I can tell you that in a couple of words," Bridgwater replied. "His two nephews. And that is the last thing Matthew would have wanted."

"Had Sir Matthew no other relatives?" Arnold asked.

"His only other relative was George, and he, it appears is dead," Bridgwater replied.

"I can assure you that Mr. George Hawken is dead," said Arnold. "I will give you some particulars regarding his death later on. What is the present position regarding Sir Matthew's estate?"

"That I will endeavour to explain," Bridgwater replied. "The estate is considerable. It consists first of the collection of pictures, which Matthew always valued very highly. Then this property and securities amounting to roughly fifty thousand pounds. Some years ago Matthew made a will, leaving the pictures to his brother George, the property and thirty thousand pounds to Miss Paris, and the residue to Albert Oakley. There was no mention in the will of either of the nephews."

"Was there any reason for their exclusion?" Arnold asked.

"It was merely that Matthew had very little use for either of them," Bridgwater replied. "He considered Hubert to be a pompous ass, and Barry to be a vagabond. He told me at the time the will was being drawn up that Hubert had enough money already, and that if Barry were left any, he would merely pour it down the drain.

"Matthew signed the will in my office, and his signature was witnessed by two of my clerks. I and my junior partner were appointed executors. I offered to keep the will in my strong-room, but Matthew insisted on retaining it in his own possession. He brought it back here, and locked it up in the deed-box in which he kept his papers.

"Now Miss Paris tells me that, shortly after receiving the news of his brother's death, Matthew destroyed the will in her presence. A most imprudent action, in my opinion. The will might have been allowed to remain in existence until Matthew had made a fresh one, as he intended to do. But he said there was no hurry about that, and that it could await my return. So Matthew died intestate, and the estate will be shared by his two nephews in equal shares. Which seems very hard luck on Miss Paris and Albert Oakley."

"It is indeed," Arnold agreed. "Now, Mr. Bridgwater, in return for the information which you have given me, I will tell you about the death of Mr. George Hawken."

Bridgwater listened to Arnold's account with the greatest interest. "Since you were summoned by the local police I gather that it is possible that George's death was not accidental?"

"Strictly between ourselves, my own opinion is that it was a case of murder," Arnold replied. "And I believe that the murderer took a sum of money from Cliff Cottage. It is known that Barry Benson was in financial straits at the time. He came here a few days earlier to try to persuade Sir Matthew to give him some money, but Sir Matthew refused to see him. Further, it seems most significant that Barry, by his own contrivance, was in the neighbourhood of Port Bosun at the time of his uncle's death. He has not shown up since, and so far all our efforts to trace him have failed."

"Had Barry anything to gain by the death of his Uncle George?" Bridgwater asked.

"He had," Arnold replied. "Mr. George Hawken had made a will, leaving his pictures to his brother, and Cliff Cottage and its contents to Barry."

"Miss Paris told me about the pictures," said Bridgwater. "In fact I have seen them for myself. They look pretty queer stuff to me, but then I don't know much about art. Miss Paris says that Matthew greatly admired them. In fact, he maintained that his brother was a better artist than he was himself. That may be so, but George never made the reputation that Matthew did. In his day, Matthew was the most popular of all portrait painters, and was able to command a very good price for his work."

"So I understand," Arnold replied. "You will attend the inquest to-morrow, Mr. Bridgwater?"

"I certainly shall," Bridgwater said. "Hubert has undertaken to drive me to London this evening, and to bring me down again in the morning. There's no room for us to stay here in this barn."

"Then we shall meet again," said Arnold. "We need not keep you any longer now, Mr. Bridgwater. We will come out with you and have a word with Mr. Hubert."

The three of them left the pantry and went out on to the terrace. They found Hubert and Francine sitting there, and it seemed to Arnold that Hubert looked very annoyed about something. He looked up as the three men approached.

"We've met before, Mr. Arnold," he said. "I remember you coming to my office not so long ago asking for Barry. I have heard nothing of him since then."

"Perhaps he will turn up when he hears of Sir Matthew's death," Arnold replied. "You got the news yesterday, I believe?"

"That is correct," said Hubert. "And you can imagine what a shock it was to me. It seems only yesterday that I had to break the news of his brother's death to Uncle Matthew. And then came Francine's telegram informing me of Uncle Matthew's death. The family of Hawken has become extinct."

"You came here as soon as you could after the receipt of the telegram from Miss Paris?" Arnold asked.

"I couldn't get away before lunch-time to-day," Hubert replied. "As I told you before, Mr. Arnold, I am a busy man. I was hard at work in my office when Francine's telegram came, and I had a most important appointment this morning. I couldn't have done any good here if I had come down earlier."

"That is quite true, Mr. Benson," said Filland. "But you will understand that, as Sir Matthew's only available relative, you will be called upon to give evidence of identification at the inquest to-morrow?"

"I am prepared to do that," Hubert replied. "When and where is the inquest to be held?"

"At half-past two in the Greyhound," said Filland. "The club-room there is the only suitable place in the village."

"We shall meet there," said Arnold. "Until then, we will say good-bye."

Chapter VII

Arnold and Filland walked down to the car and got into it. "You'd like to go back to Dersham, Mr. Arnold?" Filland asked.

"I'd like to call at the vicarage first," Arnold replied. "It is possible that a friend of mine is staying there, and I should like to see him. I won't keep you waiting long."

"That will be all right," said Filland as they started off. "By the way, I can tell you something about Charlie Potter. Oakley was quite right when he called him a proper tippler. Jarrow, the constable stationed in Shepherd Green has had a lot of trouble with him. When he's had several drinks, he gets obscene and abusive. Jarrow warned him many times, but at last he lost patience with him. One evening when Charlie was particularly obstreperous, Jarrow locked him up. He came before the Bench at Dersham in the morning, charged with being drunk and disorderly. The chairman gave him a lecture and fined him two pounds. Since then, we haven't heard so much of him."

"I'll see him some time," Arnold replied. "If he was at Moat Barn yesterday morning he may have seen or heard something."

They reached the vicarage, and Arnold alighted, leaving Filland in the car. He rang the bell, and Mrs. Welback opened the door. "Is Mr. Dedham at home?" Arnold asked.

"Yes, sir," Mrs. Welback replied. "Mr. Dedham is in the drawing-room with Mr. and Mrs. Merrion, who are staying here. Will you tell me your name, please?"

Arnold told her, and she led him to the drawing-room. Luke and the Merrions were having tea, and rose with one accord as Arnold came in.

"This is indeed a pleasure, Mr. Arnold!" Luke claimed. "You will remember our meeting the last time you were at Moat Barn? You need no introduction to my friends here."

"This is not entirely unexpected," said Merrion. "One assumes that Sir Matthew's death has brought you here?"

"That is quite correct," Arnold replied. "I have just come from Moat Barn."

"Before we go any further," said Luke. "Are you going back

to London this evening, Mr. Arnold?"

Arnold shook his head. "It's hardly worth while, as I shall have to be here to-morrow. Inspector Filland, who drove me here, tells me that I can put up at the Kettledrum in Dersham."

"You'll do nothing of the kind, Mr. Arnold," said Luke firmly. "You'll stay here with me. There are plenty of rooms in this rambling old house, and it does them good to be used occasionally. We may take that as settled?"

"That is more than kind of you, Mr. Dedham," Arnold replied. "I shall enjoy nothing better. I've got a suitcase in Filland's car. I'll go and fetch it, and tell him where I'm to be found if I'm wanted."

After dinner that evening, Luke and this three guests sat together in the drawing-room. Luke had offered Arnold and Merrion the use of his study, but Arnold had declined the offer.

"We don't want to shut ourselves away," he had said. "I shall be glad of any comment upon what I have to say, and your local knowledge will be of the greatest value to me, Mr. Dedham."

So, seated in the drawing-room, Arnold repeated the conversations he had had at Moat Barn.

"I'm concerned first with opportunity," he went on. "At lunch, Albert Oakley served the portions in the kitchen, out of sight of Sir Matthew and Miss Paris. He could have added poison to the portion he brought to Sir Matthew. During lunch, Miss Paris could hardly have poisoned Sir Matthew's food. But afterwards, under pretence of giving Sir Matthew his accustomed digestive tablet, she could instead have given him a poisonous tablet which she had prepared. I do not see who else could have poisoned Sir Matthew.

"Then we come to the baffling question of motive. Had Sir Matthew died before he destroyed his existing will, both Miss Paris and Oakley would have benefited by his death. But, as things are, Sir Matthew died intestate and the only people who gain financially by his death are his two nephews. You may attribute motive to them, but not opportunity. Hubert says that he was in his London office at the time of his uncle's death, and his alibi can easily be verified. Barry is apparently in hiding. He can hardly have been at Moat Barn yesterday, without being seen either by Miss Paris or Albert Oakley. On the whole I am inclined to suspect Miss Paris, in spite of the fact that her motive is obscure. What can you tell me about her, Mr. Dedham?"

Luke looked slightly uncomfortable. "I refuse to believe that Francine is a murderess," he replied. "But I can tell you how she came to take the post of nurse to Sir Matthew. As you know, he was at one time a distinguished portrait painter. Not only that, but he painted other pictures as well, employing models. His favourite model was a certain Vanessa. I'm talking about a long while ago, and I never heard what her surname was then. Mr. Bridgwater could probably tell you, for he knew Sir Matthew long before I did. I have been told that there was some talk of Sir Matthew marrying Vanessa. But he never did, and she married a Frenchman, Jules Paris, instead.

"Some years later Sir Matthew bought the building now known as Moat Barn. It had been the parish tithe barn, set up on the mound so that it would run no risk of being flooded. But tithes in kind had become obsolete, and the building had fallen into disrepair. Sir Matthew had it repaired and converted to his own liking. The drawbridge was one of his so-called improvements. For some time Sir Matthew lived there with Albert Oakley as his cook, valet and sole attendant.

"Then Sir Matthew had a stroke, from which he recovered partially paralysed. It was obvious that he would have to have a nurse, and Dick Kent offered to find him one. But Sir Matthew said that be believed he could find one for himself. His former model, Vanessa, had a widowed sister, Hilda Retford, who was a trained nurse. He would get in touch with her, and ask her to come and live at Moat Barn.

"Mrs. Retford did come, and highly efficient she proved to be. But after a few years her brother, a bachelor, developed a chronic illness and needed constant attention. Mrs. Retford had to choose between Sir Matthew, of whom she had grown very fond, and her brother. She decided that her brother had the greater claim on her, and, I think very reluctantly, she left Moat Barn and joined her brother in the north of England.

"But, before she did so, she had found someone to take her place. Her sister and Jules Paris were both dead. But they had a daughter, Francine, who had been trained as a nurse and was then on the staff of a hospital, where she was not particularly happy. Mrs. Retford sent for Francine and introduced her to Sir Matthew, who took to her on the spot. He told me later that Francine was the image of her mother, as she had been at her daughter's age.

"He must have been right about that. While you were in the studio you may have noticed the nymphs in some of Sir Matthew's pictures. Vanessa sat as the model for them, and the likeness to Francine is striking. Sir Matthew had given up painting before Francine came to him, otherwise, I am sure, he would have painted her. In spite of the disparity in their ages, Sir Matthew and Francine became devoted to each other. In fact, it would be difficult to find three people who got on so well together as did Sir Matthew, Francine and Albert Oakley."

"Sir Matthew was not very approachable, I gather?" Arnold asked.

Luke smiled. "The drawbridge is sufficient evidence of that. But you mustn't run away with the idea that he was a hermit. He was always ready to see anyone he liked. Dick Kent and myself, for instance. He would talk to us quite freely and entertainingly. But the drawbridge was an effectual barrier against those whom he didn't want to see."

"Mrs. Aintree is very resentful of the fact that Sir Matthew would never see her," Mavis remarked. "She seems to think that, since he had once painted her portrait, she had a claim upon his affections."

"Yes, I know," Luke replied. "But, with the exception of Francine, Sir Matthew didn't care for the company of women. Amabel Aintree isn't the only one against whom the drawbridge is raised. Francine told me that Christine, Hubert's wife, drove down to Moat Barn one day last week. But, even though she was his niece by marriage, Sir Matthew wouldn't see her. He told Francine that Christine had no business to come down uninvited."

"What can you tell me about Sir Matthew's two nephews?" Arnold asked.

"I have never been well acquainted with either of them," Luke replied. "Nor did I ever meet their parents. Eleanor Hawken, who came between her two brothers, married before the First War. Her husband was rich, and he and Eleanor looked down on Matthew and George, struggling and unknown artists.

Later the Benson couple did their best to curry favour with Matthew, but he would have none of it. He never forgave their earlier attitude towards him. Which may in part account for his lack of affection for their two sons.

"You must understand that I am only repeating what Sir Matthew told me from time to time. His dislike of his nephews may have prejudiced him where they were concerned. Both their parents died before Sir Matthew became incapacitated. He attended his sister's funeral, her husband had pre-deceased her. Since then, both nephews have been invited to Moat Barn, but only at long intervals, and only for the day. That explains why I have so little personal knowledge of either of them.

"Robert Benson left Eleanor an income for life, with reversion to Hubert, the older son. The rest he left to Hubert to the complete exclusion of Barry. Hubert made the best use of his money. He took over the business in the City which had been his father's and, from all accounts, he has done very well out of it. He and Christine live in the best part of Wimbledon, on the grand scale. They entertain lavishly, and they each have a car, which they exchange for a new one at frequent intervals. Hubert may be described as a highly successful businessman."

"I called on him at his office not long ago," said Arnold. "His business is that of an import and export merchant."

"Exactly," Luke replied. "His business constantly takes Hubert abroad, and I believe that Christine usually goes with him. He was in France at the time of his Uncle George's death, I understand."

"He was," said Arnold. "His secretary wrote to him there, but it was a day or two before he received the letter. I can't say that I care much for Hubert Benson. His manner is too abrupt for my liking. What is your opinion of his brother?"

"I have seen very little of him," Luke replied. "But, on that slight acquaintance, I like him better than I do his brother. Barry may be a vagabond, but he strikes me as being more genuine than Hubert. Sir Matthew used to say that if his father had left Barry some of his money, he would have had a start in life and might have stuck to it. As it was, he had to take the first job that came along. He has drifted from one job to another, never sticking to any of them for long."

"Did Hubert never offer his brother a helping hand?" Arnold

asked.

Luke shook his head. "Not to my knowledge. And I don't think it's likely that he ever did. He is far from being the soul of generosity, in spite of the fact that he must be a wealthy man."

"Which is more than Barry is ever likely to become," said Arnold. "His Uncle George must have had a not wholly unfavourable opinion of him. He had appointed Barry one of his executors. Since Barry is not to be found, the other executor has performed the duties. His is Mr. Paul Clapdale, a friend of Mr. George Hawken. By the way, do you know that Sir Matthew had a visitor yesterday morning?"

"Yes, I know that," Luke replied. "Francine told me."

"There is something mysterious about that visitor," said Arnold. "Sir Matthew must have been expecting him, or he would not have received him. It seems rather strange that he had not told Miss Paris of the impending visit. The visitor would not tell Albert Oakley his name. He said that Sir Matthew would know him when he saw him. He is described as a short man, dressed all in black. The interview between him and Sir Matthew ended in something approaching a quarrel. Sir Matthew ordered his visitor off the premises.

"Naturally, I should like to know who this visitor was. He showed Albert one of Sir Matthew's cards, with a date and time written on it in Sir Matthew's handwriting. It seems certain, therefore, that he had written to Sir Matthew asking for an appointment, and that Sir Matthew had granted him one. No doubt his letter could be found among Sir Matthew's papers?"

"I very much doubt it," Luke replied. "Sir Matthew had a habit of tearing up the letters he received as soon as he had answered them."

"He was capable of answering his own letters?" Arnold asked.

"Oh, quite," Luke replied, "although he was partially paralysed, his brain was in no way affected. When he wanted to write a letter, Francine pushed him in his chair up to a table, on which he wrote. Either Francine or Albert posted it for him in the village. It is unlikely that either of them would be sufficiently inquisitive to read the address on the envelope."

"So I shan't get the visitor's name by making inquiries at Moat Barn," said Arnold. "But I have an idea who he may have been. I'll tell you a rather curious thing. About four weeks before his death, Mr. George Hawken had a visitor, dressed all in black. Mr. Clapdale saw the two of them together at Cliff Cottage. Mr. Hawken subsequently told Mr. Clapdale that his visitor had been an art dealer of the name of Green, and that he had bought two of his pictures at a satisfactory price. It seems to me that this Green may have been the man who called at Moat Barn yesterday."

"That seems quite possible," Luke agreed. "Green asked for an appointment to see Sir Matthew's pictures. He may have wanted to buy one or two of them, but the price he offered seemed to Sir Matthew entirely inadequate. Hence the quarrel."

"I don't see why you should worry your head about Green," said Merrion. "You can't be certain yet that he was yesterday's visitor to Moat Barn. I'll agree that if he was, he seems to be a bird of ill omen. Both Hawken brothers died soon after his visits to them. But it seems impossible that Green should have poisoned Sir Matthew. In any case, why should he have wanted to?"

"I can answer that question," Arnold replied. "He expected that on Sir Matthew's death his pictures would be sold by auction. If that happened, he hoped to buy what he wanted cheaply."

"Very well," said Merrion. "We will allow the man a motive. But where was his opportunity?"

"He was in the studio not long before Sir Matthew had his lunch," Arnold replied.

"Yes, but he wasn't alone there," said Merrion.

"And at the time Sir Matthew's lunch was being prepared in the kitchen. Even my imagination can't see any way in which he could have administered the poison. The only two people who had that opportunity were Miss Paris and Albert."

"I won't have it!" Luke exclaimed. "They were both devoted to Sir Matthew."

"Then where else is Arnold to look?" Merrion asked. "Perhaps the answer to that is Port Bosun."

"And what do you mean by that?" Arnold demanded.

"I will try to explain," Merrion replied. "I cannot believe that the death of Sir Matthew was an isolated event. It followed too closely on the death of his brother. I am inclined to the opinion that both Hawken brothers were murdered, and by the same hand."

Arnold shook his head. "It won't do. I am practically satisfied that Mr. George Hawken was murdered by his nephew Barry. And Barry cannot possibly have been at Moat Barn yesterday without the knowledge of either Miss Paris or Albert."

"You are practically satisfied," said Merrion. "But you can't be certain. I will admit that appearances are very much against Barry, but that is not definite proof that he is a murderer. To get back to yesterday. Was anyone at Moat Barn during the morning besides the people you have told us about?"

"Only the gardener, Charlie Potter," Arnold replied. "He was there for a short time in the morning, and said he was coming back in the afternoon, but apparently he didn't. From what I hear he seems to be rather a disreputable character. I expect you know all about him, Mr. Dedham?"

"I do indeed," said Luke. "He is, I regret to say, the black sheep of my flock. I don't think that there is any real vice in him, but he gets drunk and makes a nuisance of himself. I will say this in his favour. He is a most excellent gardener when he chooses to work."

"Is he a married man with a family?" Arnold asked.

"He has never been married," Luke replied. "He lives by himself in a tiny cottage. He has a married sister, who goes out to work by the day for a family in the village. She cleans out Charlie's cottage for him when she can find the time."

"Charlie was at Moat Barn this morning," said Arnold. "He told Albert that someone had stolen his smock and apron."

Luke smiled. "Being familiar with Charlie's smock and apron, it doesn't seem to me very likely that anyone stole them. They are no better than rags. It is far more likely that Charlie mislaid his property when he was under the influence of drink."

"Is anyone else employed at Moat Barn?" Merrion asked.

"Yes," Luke replied. "Mrs. Toogood, the wife of our local cobbler. She goes to Moat Barn three afternoons a week, to help Albert with the scrubbing. Her days at Moat Barn are Tuesday, Thursday and Friday, but she may have been there yesterday afternoon. She's an honest, hardworking woman, though her appearance is rather striking."

"In what way?" Arnold asked.

"In her attire," Luke replied. "She wears the strangest hat, indoor and out. It goes up in stages, like a wedding cake, and is wreathed in roses, cherries, and lilies of the valley, artificial, of course. She picks up these decorations at jumble sales, and is immensely proud of them."

"Had Mrs. Toogood any motive for murdering Sir Matthew?" Merrion asked. "If she was at Moat Barn on Tuesday afternoon, she could have added poison to the food in the larder."

"She can't have done that," Arnold replied. "If she had, there would have been three victims. I am told that Sir Matthew was not on an invalid diet. He ate the same food as Miss Paris and Albert. That is so, is it not, Mr. Dedham?"

"So Dick Kent has told me," Luke replied. "He said that there was no reason why Sir Matthew should not eat what he likes. It was probable that it was more convenient for Albert to prepare one meal for the three of them. As for Mrs. Toogood having any motive for murdering Sir Matthew, I cannot imagine what it could have been."

"I think we can eliminate Mrs. Toogood," said Arnold. "And, for that matter, all those who formed Sir Matthew's household. As things stood, none of them had any motive. But, if Sir Matthew was murdered, as I have very little doubt that he was, the motive may not have been a financial one. Is any other motive, such as revenge, possible?"

"I know of no one who could have had such a motive," Luke replied. "I have never heard of Sir Matthew having injured anyone. Of course he may have done so long ago, before he came to live at Moat Barn."

"Resentment is sometimes long lived," Merrion remarked. "By the way, has any announcement of Sir Matthew's death been made?"

"When Francine came to see me yesterday, I suggested to her that she should insert a notice in the Deaths column of The Times" Luke replied. "She said that she didn't know the proper way to make it out. I said that I would write out a notice and post it to The Times. I did so, and it should appear to-morrow."

Chapter VIII

The inquest was held on Friday afternoon in the club-room attached to the Greyhound. This was the room in which the cricket teams had tea. For many years past the Shepherd Green team had been photographed at the end of the season. The club-room was hung with copies of these photographs, some of them so faded as to be almost indiscernible.

A trestle table had been set up at one end of the room, and chairs ranged round it. The rest of the space was occupied with rows of benches, for the convenience of the general public. The foremost row was reserved for the witnesses. The party from the vicarage arrived on the scene in good time, to find Dick Kent and Filland already here. Francine and Albert arrived together shortly afterwards. They were shortly followed by the pathologist, who drove up in his car. Finally the coroner arrived, also in a car.

Jarrow had got together a jury of four men and three women, who were accommodated on a couple of benches beside the table. The coroner set to work without delay. The jury elected as their foreman Mr. Glynde, the village grocer, and were sworn in.

The first witness called was Hubert Benson, who had driven Mr. Bridgwater down from London. Jarrow led him to a chair beside the coroner's. Hubert gave his name and described himself as a merchant. He had seen the body, and recognised it as that of his uncle, aged eighty-four and single, Sir Matthew Hawken, who had lived at Moat Barn in the parish of Shepherd Green. In reply to the coroner, the witness said that he had last seen his uncle alive some weeks earlier. He had then seemed in fairly good health, but he had been greatly shocked by the death of his brother. This, no doubt, had had a depressing effect upon his mind.

Francine took Hubert's place. She gave her name, and described herself as a private nurse. She had been in attendance on the deceased for the past seven years. The deceased, although partly paralysed, enjoyed exceptionally good health for a man of his age. On Wednesday morning he had seemed quite well and in good spirits.

The coroner intervened with a question. Had the deceased entirely recovered from the shock of his brother's death? To which Francine replied that to all appearances he had. He had certainly been greatly depressed for a few days after hearing the news, but that depression seemed to have gradually passed away.

Francine went on to describe how she and Sir Matthew had had lunch together. After lunch she had given him his usual digestive tablet, and helped him into bed. This had been the normal routine. Sir Matthew usually slept for an hour or so, but on this occasion he did not wake at the end of this time. After waiting for what seemed to be a reasonable time the witness had endeavoured to rouse him, but without success. She had therefore sent for Dr. Kent.

The medical evidence was then taken. Dick Kent described how he had been summoned to Moat Barn on Wednesday afternoon. As soon as he arrived there he had examined the deceased to find that he was dead. In his opinion, death had occurred between an hour and two hours previously. This suggested that the deceased had died very soon after getting into bed. Some time previously the deceased had complained of mild indigestion. The witness had therefore prescribed tablets, one to be taken after each meal. The tablets were of five grains each, and consisted mainly of magnesium carbonate. There was nothing in them which could have been in any way harmful. Since there were no external appearances to account for the death of the deceased, the witness had informed the coroner.

The pathologist took the chair vacated by Dick Kent. At the coroner's request he, in conjunction with the previous witness, had carried out a post-mortem examination. The condition of the organs strongly suggested the presence of some poisonous substance. The witness had removed the contents of the stomach and submitted them to analysis. The results of this had been to show the presence of a cyanide, probably potassium cyanide, in considerable quantity. The poison had been swallowed in solid form.

Asked by the coroner if he could estimate how much of the poison had been swallowed, the witness said that he thought that the quantity had been about four or five grains. It would be difficult to lay down the quantity of potassium cyanide which would prove fatal, as it varied widely with different individuals. A case was on record where two grains had caused death, and another where the patient had recovered after swallowing fifty grains. It was generally recognised that a dose of four or five grains was likely to cause death. The witness stated that he personally would expect that amount, or even less, to be fatal to a man of the age of the deceased.

The coroner asked how soon after taking the poison death would ensue. The witness replied that it was difficult to say, but that he thought ten minutes would be a rough estimate. Taking into account the estimate of the time of death by the previous witness, it seemed to be established that the deceased must have taken the poison during or after his lunch. Certainly not before.

The coroner recalled Francine and questioned her. Was any potassium cyanide kept at Moat Barn? She replied that to the best of her knowledge none had ever been kept there. The only poison on the premises was a tin of rat poison, which was kept in one of the outhouses. The coroner then asked her how soon after finishing his lunch was the deceased in bed? She replied in less than five minutes. She had helped him to take off his outer clothes. Then she had given him a tablet from the box on the bedside table, which he had swallowed down with a few drops of wine which he had left in his glass for the purpose. She had then helped him into bed. Asked if she had remained with the deceased after he was in bed, she replied that she had not. She had gone to her room, leaving the door open so that she could hear the deceased if he called. She was sure that he had not called. If he had, either she or Albert Oakley would have heard him.

Albert was the last witness. He described how he had cooked and served lunch on Wednesday. When Sir Matthew and Miss Paris had had their lunch, he had had his; exactly the same as they had had, but for the wine. While he was clearing the table in the studio, he had seen Miss Paris take a tablet from the box and give it to Sir Matthew. He had then seen her help him into bed. When he had finished clearing the table, he had had his lunch in the kitchen, leaving the door open so that he could hear Sir Matthew if he wanted anything. He had heard no sound from Sir Matthew.

Questioned by the coroner, Albert said that he had no knowledge of any potassium being in the house. The only poison that he knew about was the tin of rat poison of which Miss Paris had spoken. They sometimes had rats round the outhouses, and the witness was in the habit of laying poisoned bait for them.

This concluded the evidence, and the coroner addressed the jury. The medical evidence left no doubt as to the cause of death. What the jury must consider was how and in what form the deceased had taken the poison. Accident was not easy to imagine. If the food consumed at lunch had accidentally become contaminated, one or both of the other partakers of the meal would have been affected. It was clear from the evidence that the deceased must have swallowed the poison either during lunch or after it.

The evidence as to the state of the deceased's mind was slightly contradictory. One witness had testified that he was greatly distressed by the death of his brother. Another, and one who had had the deceased under constant observation, had said that this depression had passed. It might be however that it had merely been repressed, and that it still affected the mind of the deceased. The jury should consider the possibility of suicide, though they would have to face the difficult question of how the deceased could have obtained the poison, and how he could have taken it without the knowledge of his attendants.

There remained only the possibility of foul play. It would be for the jury to decide whether or not some person had administered the poison with the deliberate intention of causing the death of the deceased. They were at liberty to retire if they wished to do so.

After consultation with his colleagues, Mr. Glynde announced that they wished to retire. They rose and Mr. Glynde led them from the club-room into the inn parlour. They were absent for just upon an hour, which suggested that they had difficulty in arriving at a unanimous verdict. At last they returned and resumed their seats, looking very uncomfortable. In reply to the coroner's question, Mr. Glynde said haltingly that they were agreed upon their verdict. It was that Sir Matthew had died as the result of swallowing poison deliberately administered by some person unknown.

The coroner intimated that he did not disagree with that verdict. He understood that the police were already investigating the matter. It was profoundly to be hoped that they would succeed in unmasking the criminal. He would like to express his deep sympathy with the relatives of the deceased. He made out a burial certificate, and handed it to Hubert, who promptly passed it on to Mr Bridgwater. With that, the proceedings ended.

Luke and the Merrions walked back to the vicarage, while Arnold remained in consultation with Filland and Jarrow.

"I think I saw Mrs. Toogood, who works at Moat Barn, in court," said Arnold. "Her hat has been described to me, and I'm sure I recognised it. Am I right, Constable?"

"That's quite right, sir," Jarrow replied. "She was there, and I saw her going off towards Moat Barn a couple of minutes ago."

"Was Charlie Potter in court?" Arnold asked.

"I don't think so, sir," Jarrow replied. "But I saw him just before the inquest started. He came out of the Greyhound, and when he saw me he came up and began moaning about somebody having stolen the clothes he worked in. I didn't take any notice of him. For one thing I was too busy, and for another Charlie doesn't always know what he's talking about when he's had one or two."

"I should like a word with Charlie," said Arnold. "I'm told that he was at Moat Barn on Wednesday morning. Do you suppose that he'd be sober enough to answer a few questions?"

"He should be at this time, sir," Jarrow replied. "I'll show you where he lives, if you like."

He led Arnold and Filland to a small and dilapidated cottage at the edge of the village. The door was shut, and Jarrow rapped upon it smartly. A hoarse voice from within replied, "Come in, whoever you are. The door is not locked. You have only got to lift the latch."

Jarrow did so, and the three walked in. The door opened into the kitchen, where an elderly man was sitting at the table, turning over the pages of a seed catalogue. He was wearing no coat, and displayed a grimy flannel shirt and an equally grimy pair of corduroy trousers.

"Why, if it isn't Mr. Jarrow!" he exclaimed. "And who have you brought with you, Mr. Jarrow?"

"We are police officers," Arnold replied. "And we have come to ask you a question or two. You were at Moat Barn on Wednesday morning, I believe?"

"That's right," said Charlie. "It's where I used to work most days. But I shan't go there any more. How am I to know who'll pay my wages now that Sir Matthew's dead?"

"Did you see any strangers about when you were at Moat Barn that morning?" Arnold asked.

"I didn't see no strangers," Charlie replied. "I didn't see nobody but Albert Oakley. I told him it was too wet for me to do any work. I said I'd get along, and that I might come back in the afternoon if the weather cleared up. But I didn't."

"Where did you go after you left Moat Barn?" Arnold asked.

"Why, along to the Greyhound for a pint," Charlie replied. "Then I came back here. And it wasn't long after that that the black man came along."

"The black man?" Arnold exclaimed. "Do you mean a man dressed all in black?"

"I mean what I say," Charlie replied. "A black man. A nigger with black face and hands. He was wearing an old cap, pulled right down over his eyes, and a light coloured raincoat. My smock and apron were wet, so I'd hung them up to dry. I hadn't shut the door, and this chap just walked right in."

"You asked him what his business was, I suppose?" Arnold asked.

"I did, straight," Charlie replied. "I asked him what he meant by walking in on me like that. He said that he'd got something for me. He took a bottle wrapped in paper out of his raincoat pocket, and put it down on the table in front of me.

"Naturally I asked him where it came from. He said he'd just been to Moat Barn, and that Sir Matthew had asked him to take me a bottle of whisky in celebration of cricket week. I took the paper from the bottle and sure enough it was a bottle of whisky. It was full and had never been opened. Then the chap said he hoped I'd enjoy it and went off."

This seemed to Arnold a most improbable story. He turned to Jarrow. "Have you heard of a black man being seen about the village on Wednesday?" he asked.

"No, sir, I haven't," Jarrow replied. "And I don't believe there was one, else I should have heard of him."

Arnold returned to Charlie. "What happened next?" he asked.

"Why, I opened the bottle and had a tot," Charlie replied. "I like a drop of whisky now and again, though it's mostly beer I drink. It was rare good whisky, and I had another tot, and maybe one or two more after that I must have dozed off, and it was the middle of the afternoon before I came to. I saw that the door was shut, though the black man had left it open when he went out. And then I saw that the smock and apron that I'd hung up were missing. Somebody must have come in and taken them while I was asleep. It's a job for the police, that's what I say."

"We'll do our best to find your property for you," said Arnold. "You didn't go back to Moat Barn that afternoon?"

Charlie shook his head. "I didn't feel much like work. Besides, the ground was too wet. There was a little whisky left in the bottle, so I finished that."

"What did you do with the empty bottle?" Arnold asked.

"Chucked it into the dust bin," Charlie replied. You'll find it there now if you want it. Come and I'll show you."

The dust bin stood outside the cottage door. Charlie led them to it and took off the lid. Sure enough, half-buried in refuse was a whisky bottle. Arnold took it out and examined the label, which bore the word, "Piebald Horse Brand. Finest Scotch."

"You had better take charge of that, Constable," said Arnold, as they started off towards the centre of the village. "What do you think of Charlie's story?"

"It doesn't make sense, sir," Jarrow replied. "Charlie must have dreamt it."

"Then where did the bottle of whisky come from?" Arnold asked.

"Charlie might have bought it at the Greyhound, sir," Jarrow replied. "There's nowhere else in the village where one can buy spirits."

"We'll go and ask," said Arnold. They walked to the Greyhound, to find the door locked at that time in the afternoon. However, Jarrow hammered on it, and after an interval it was unlocked and the landlord appeared.

"Good afternoon, gentlemen," he said. "I'm just trying to get the club-room in order again. What is it you want of me?"

"We shan't keep you more than a minute," Arnold replied. "Did Charlie Potter buy a bottle of whisky from you on Wednesday?"

The landlord shook his head. "He was here that morning. I recollect him saying that it was too wet for him to work at Moat Barn. He had a pint or two of old and mild, but he didn't ask for any whisky. He may have a double now and again, but he's never bought a whole bottle."

"Do you stock a brand known as Piebald Horse?" Arnold asked.

"No, I don't," the landlord replied. "None of my customers ever ask for it. Of course I have to take what the brewers send, but I've never had any Piebald Horse in the house."

"Thank you," said Arnold. "We'll let you get on with your work now."

"Where would you like to go now, Mr. Arnold?" Filland asked as they walked away from the inn.

"I'd like a few words with Mrs. Toogood," Arnold replied. "You can show us where she lives, Constable."

Jarrow led them a few yards along the village street to the cobbler's shop. The door was open, and they walked in.

"Good afternoon, gentlemen," said the man behind the counter, "Any shoes to repair?"

"Not for the moment," Arnold replied. "We should like to see Mrs. Toogood, if she's at home."

"You'll find her in the kitchen," said Toogood. He opened a door at the back of the shop. "Mr. Jarrow and two gentlemen to see you, Ellen. There you are. Go through."

They passed into the kitchen where Mrs. Toogood, still wearing her preposterous hat, was busy ironing.

"Good afternoon, Mrs. Toogood," said Arnold. "Will you tell us when you last saw Sir Matthew Hawken?"

She looked at him mistrustfully. "And who might you be that calls me by my name?" she replied.

Jarrow interposed tactfully. "The gentleman is Inspector Arnold from Scotland Yard. You needn't make any difficulty about answering his questions, Mrs. Toogood."

Her eyes brightened with interest. "Scotland Yard!" she exclaimed. "Well I never! When did I last see Sir Matthew? Why, on Tuesday morning, to be sure. Tuesday is one of my regular mornings for going to Moat Barn. When it's fine I always sweep over the terrace. It's wonderful how the dust always seems to settle there. And when I started to do that on Tuesday, Sir Matthew was sitting out there. He was always such a pleasant gentleman, and he asked me how my husband was. You see, he'd been suffering from a pain in his back. I told Sir Matthew that he was doing fairly, thank you, and that Dr. Kent had seen him and said it was nothing serious. Then Sir Matthew said that I needn't do any more sweeping, as the dust was blowing into his eyes. So I went into the house and cleaned up in the studio. It was a good chance, as Sir Matthew wasn't there."

It was evident that once Mrs. Toogood was started, it would be difficult to stop her. But Arnold ventured on another question. "Was Sir Matthew in his usual health and spirits that day?"

"Just as he always was," Mrs. Toogood replied. "Cheerful and with a kindly word for everyone. Some weeks back he'd been terribly upset when Mr. Hubert came and told him that Mr. George was dead. But he stayed in bed and said he didn't feel strong enough to get up. After a few days he got over that and was as spry as ever."

"Were you at Moat Barn at any time on Wednesday?" Arnold asked.

Mrs. Toogood shook her head. "It wasn't my day. Sometimes I put in a couple of hours on my off days, if Miss Paris sends for me. But she didn't that day, though I saw her in the afternoon. I had gone to post a letter, and when I got to the post office Miss Paris came out and told me that Sir Matthew was dead. I supposed that he had just passed out quietly, like old men do. And when I heard just now that Sir Matthew had been poisoned, I couldn't believe my ears. Who could have done it? Not Miss Paris or Albert Oakley, that I'll swear."

"You have no suspicions?" Arnold asked.

"Suspicions?" she exclaimed. "Who could suspect anyone of wanting to murder Sir Matthew? He never did anyone any harm. And if he got to hear that anyone in the village was in trouble, he'd always put his hand in his pocket to help them. It strikes me there must be some mistake. The doctors aren't always right, though they may think they are. And what's the lady going to do now, I'd like to know?"

"Miss Paris?" Arnold asked. "I don't suppose she'll find any difficulty in securing another nursing post."

"She won't do that," Mrs. Toogood replied firmly. "I know a thing or two, but I'm keeping my mouth shut. And now, with all due respect, I'd like to be allowed to get on with my ironing."

After this pointed remark, Arnold saw no need to continue the conversation, and the three men left the house.

"I wonder what Mrs. Toogood knows or thinks she knows?" said Arnold. "Not who poisoned Sir Matthew, that I feel sure. I think it's time that we went along to Moat Barn. No need for you to come there with us, Constable."

"No need to walk," Filland replied. "I've got my car standing outside the Greyhound. We may as well drive there, Mr. Arnold."

They drove to Moat Barn, and as they pulled up a car came from round the mound and passed them. They saw that it was driven by Hubert Benson. He raised his hand in salute and drove on towards the village. The drawbridge was down, and Arnold and Filland alighted from the car and started up the path towards the house.

Albert must have seen them coming. He appeared from behind the house and approached them. "Who is here, Oakley?" Arnold asked.

"Miss Paris, Mr. Bridgwater and me," Albert replied. "Mr. Hubert said that he was too busy to stop. He's gone back to London, but he said that he'd be back for the funeral."

"No one else has been here since the inquest?" Arnold asked.

"No one, sir," Albert replied. He led them to the door which he opened. They entered the studio, to find Francine and Bridgwater seated at the table with a metal deed-box before them.

"Can we have a word with you, Miss Paris?" Arnold asked.

"By all means," she replied. "Would you like to come into my room? You will excuse me, Mr. Bridgwater?"

Bridgwater looked up from the papers he was sorting. "Certainly, certainly. We must all comply with the wishes of the police."

Francine led Arnold and Filland into her room, where they sat down. "Were you surprised by the medical evidence given at the inquest, Miss Paris?" Arnold asked.

"I was very greatly surprised," Francine replied. "And not only surprised but puzzled. I cannot imagine how Sir Matthew was poisoned, while neither Albert nor myself felt the slightest ill effects."

"You gave Sir Matthew one of the tables which Dr. Kent had prescribed for him?" Arnold asked.

"Yes," Francine replied. "I took one from the box. I don't see how the tablet can have had anything to do with it. Sir Matthew had been taking one four times a day for quite a long while past, and they had never done him any harm."

"Was the tablet you took from the box in any way different from the others that were in it?" Arnold asked.

Francine shook her head. "Not so far as I am aware. It was rather dark in the studio, and I didn't look at it very closely. I just picked out a tablet and gave it to Sir Matthew."

"Was the box visible?" Arnold asked. "By which I mean, could anyone who entered the studio have seen it?"

"It was visible, but not conspicuous," Francine replied. "It was on the table by the bed. I suppose that anyone who looked at the table would have seen it."

"Now, another thing, Miss Paris," said Arnold. "After the visitor dressed in black had gone, did anyone else from outside come here?"

"Only Dr. Kent," she replied. "Oh, yes, and Charlie Potter. As I was leaving the house to go to the village to send the telegrams, I saw him come over the bridge. I didn't actually meet him, because he didn't come up the path but turned off into the garden."

"You are quite sure that it was Charlie Potter whom you saw?" Arnold asked.

"Quite sure," Francine replied. "Nobody could mistake Charlie's smock and apron. And he was wearing a filthy old cap, which he had pulled right down over his ears. I wasn't surprised to see him, because Albert had told me that he had been here that morning, and said that he might come back in the afternoon."

"He had no regular hours for coming to work here?" Arnold asked.

"Oh, no," she replied. "He came and went as it pleased him.

Every Saturday he told Sir Matthew how many hours he had worked during the week and Sir Matthew paid him for them."

"Was Charlie strictly honest about that?" Arnold asked.

"Albert and I wondered about that," Francine replied. "So one week Albert watched when Charlie came and went and noted down the times. On Saturday Charlie's total of the hours he had been here agreed with Albert's. So we came to the conclusion that Charlie was honest enough in that respect at least."

"Did Charlie ever come into the house?" Arnold asked.

"Quite often," Francine replied. "He used to bring in vegetables from the garden and give them to Albert. Then if Sir Matthew was in the studio on Saturday, Charlie would come in to get his money."

"Did Charlie come into the house on Wednesday morning?" Arnold asked.

"He may have, after I had gone out," she replied. "Albert could probably tell you."

"Just one thing more, Miss Paris," said Arnold. "Am I to gather that you and Mr. Bridgwater were looking through Sir Matthew's papers when we interrupted you?"

"We were," Francine replied. "Mr. Bridgwater said that we ought to in case there was anything among them that needed attention."

"Have you found anything to throw light on the identity of the visitor who came here on Wednesday morning?" Arnold asked.

Francine shook her head. "Nothing. There are no letters, which is what I expected. Sir Matthew always tore up any letters which he received as soon as he had answered them. The only papers in the box are business ones. There is nothing whatever relating to Sir Matthew's private affairs."

Arnold rose to his feet and Filland followed his example. "Thank you, Miss Paris," said Arnold. "May we go into the kitchen and see Albert?"

"I don't think you'll find him there," she replied. "A minute or two before you came I asked him to go into the village and see Mr. Neate about the funeral. He is the village carpenter, and he does undertaking work as well. I am sure Sir Matthew would have liked us to employ him."

"Then we will not interrupt you any further," said Arnold.

Chapter IX

Arnold and Filland left the house and walked down the path to the car.

"I can't make out this mystery about Charlie Potter," said Arnold, as they set out towards the village. "He says that he was in a drunken stupor most of Wednesday afternoon. Miss Paris says that she saw him going |towards the garden at a time which must have been about four o'clock. What do you make of it?"

"I wouldn't put much faith in what Charlie says," Filland replied. "After drinking the best part of a bottle of whisky he was probably so drunk that he didn't know what he was doing."

"That bottle of whisky heightens the mystery," said Arnold. "Where did it come from? Charlie didn't buy it at the Greyhound. Do you suppose for a moment that it is true that a coloured man gave it to him?"

"It sounds highly unlikely," Filland replied. "And it is still more unlikely that Sir Matthew gave a coloured man a bottle of whisky to pass on to Charlie. He must have made up that yarn to account for the bottle. It strikes me as possible that he had stolen it." As they entered the village they saw Albert coining towards them. "The very man we want to see," said Arnold. "You might stop and ask him to get into the car."

Filland pulled up and beckoned. "We want a word with you, Oakley," he said. "Get into the car and we'll drive you back to Moat Barn."

Albert got in. Filland turned the car and drove slowly back along the road. "You've done your business with Mr. Neate?" Arnold asked.

"Yes, sir," Albert replied. "He said that he could have everything ready for Sir Matthew to be buried on Monday. I expect Miss Paris will arrange the time with Mr. Dedham."

"No doubt she will," said Arnold. "Is there any whisky in the cellar at Moat Barn?"

Albert looked surprised at this question. "Why, yes, sir, there is," he replied. "Sir Matthew always took a glass of whisky as a night cap. There must be at least half a dozen bottles left."

"What brand of whisky are they?" Arnold asked.

"Ptarmigan, sir," Albert replied. "That was the brand Sir Matthew liked best."

"Have you ever had any Piebald Horse brand on the premises?" Arnold asked.

Albert shook his head. "Never, sir. I have never heard of that brand."

By this time they had reached the entrance to Moat Barn, and Albert made as though to alight. But Arnold restrained him. "Don't go yet, Oakley," he said. "I've still a few questions to ask you. You are quite sure that Charlie Potter didn't come back to Moat Barn on Wednesday afternoon?"

"Well, if he did, I didn't see him, sir," Albert replied.

"When he was there in the morning, did he go into the house?" Arnold asked.

"Yes, sir, he did," Albert replied. "It was when I had gone down to speak to the gentleman in the car. When I had shown the gentleman into the studio, I went into the kitchen, and Charlie was there. He told me that he had brought in some roses for Miss Paris, and had taken them into the studio. Miss Paris wasn't there, but he had seen Sir Matthew, who had told him to put the roses on the table by the bed. Charlie must have done that, because when I came into the studio to show the gentleman out, they were there."

"Was this gentleman alone in the studio at any time?" Arnold asked.

"Only for less than a minute, sir," Albert replied. "After Sir Matthew had told him to clear out, he wheeled himself into Miss Paris's room and slammed the door behind him. I was in the gallery, and heard what Sir Matthew said. It didn't take me many seconds to come down and show the gentleman out. But of course, while I was coming down, he was alone in the studio."

"You are quite sure that Sir Matthew had no other visitor at all that morning?" Arnold asked.

"I'm quite sure about that, sir," Albert replied. "The drawbridge was down, and no one could have come in without my knowing about it."

"We have been told that there was a coloured man in the village that morning," said Arnold. "Did you by any chance see him hanging round Moat Barn?"

"A coloured man, sir?" Albert exclaimed. "I've never heard of one being in the village. No, I certainly didn't see him."

"Well, that will do now, Oakley," said Arnold. Albert alighted from the car, and Filland turned and drove back towards the village.

Meanwhile Luke Dedham and Merrion had been sitting on the vicarage lawn, discussing the evidence given at the inquest. "So our friend Arnold is faced with a clear case of murder," Merrion had said. "I don't feel inclined to quarrel with that verdict, because it seems pretty certain that Sir Matthew was murdered. But who murdered him?"

"I don't know," Luke replied miserably. "It's the most ghastly business. I hardly dare think about it."

"Arnold is bound to think about it," said Merrion. "I can't help wondering which way his thoughts will turn. He can't avoid the fact that the evidence points to one of two people having had the opportunity. Albert might have slipped some potassium cyanide into the helping of gooseberry-pie he brought to Sir Matthew. Miss Paris might have given him a tablet made of the stuff. But why?"

Luke shook his head. "Don't ask me why."

"The puzzle is that motive and opportunity pull different ways," said Merrion. "Two people had the opportunity, and two quite different people had the motive. Sir Matthew having died intestate, his estate will be shared by his two nephews. Now tell me this, Luke. If Sir Matthew had lived to make a fresh will, in whose favour would it have been?"

"Not in favour of either of his nephews," Luke replied. "I'm sure of that, because he never cared much for them. He would have left Albert a competence, no doubt. The pictures and the bulk of the estate he would have left to Francine."

"Which fixes the motive all the more firmly upon the nephews," said Merrion. "It was in their interest that Sir Matthew should die before he made such a will."

"That's true enough," Luke replied. "But, as you say yourself, neither of them had the opportunity of poisoning their uncle."

"Let's look at that a little more closely," said Merrion. "We'll go back to the death of George Hawken. Arnold believes that he was murdered, and from what he has told me of the case I think that he's probably right. And when two brothers are murdered within such a short interval, it is a fairly safe assumption that both died by the same hand."

"Hubert Benson was in France at the time of his Uncle George's death, so that he can't be suspected of the murder. But Barry was at Thramsbury, only a short distance from Port Bosun. Arnold has established that Barry had something to gain by George Hawken's death. So that in this case motive and opportunity can be attributed to the same person. Since that day, Barry has succeeded in remaining in hiding. Why should he not come forward if he were innocent?

"Then we come to the death of Sir Matthew. Hubert says that he was in London at the time, a statement which Arnold can easily verify. Where was Barry? Is it possible that he had emerged from his hiding- place and made his way to Moat Barn? I believe that it is not impossible, though I admit that it is a theory which presents many difficulties."

"It does indeed," Luke replied. "Are you quite satisfied of Francine's innocence?"

"Yes, on the score of her lack of motive," said Merrion. "But I'm not at all sure that the jury were equally satisfied. I think that some of them would have preferred a verdict implicating her. That would account for the long time it took them to reach an agreement."

With a sudden movement Luke sprang from his chair and paced the lawn from end to end before he returned to it. "Listen to me, Desmond," he said in a strained voice. "If it turned out that Francine had gained considerably by Sir Matthew's death, would you still be satisfied of her innocence?"

"No, I should not," Merrion replied. "Opportunity coupled with motive would seem to point very strongly to her guilt."

"That's the awful thing!" Luke exclaimed. "I'm going to tell you something, Desmond. It has been on my conscience night and day, ever since I heard of Sir Matthew's death. I must confide in someone, and I would rather it was you than anyone else. Now old friend, listen to me."

Merrion listened to Luke, whose voice sank until it was scarcely above a whisper. "Well, I should not have imagined that," he said when Luke had come to an end. "But what you have told me does not constitute proof of Miss Paris having poisoned Sir Matthew."

"Then you don't believe that Francine is guilty?" Luke asked eagerly.

"I appreciate that appearances are very much against her," Merrion replied. "But I am by no means convinced of her guilt. And for this reason. I am still strongly of the opinion that both brothers were murdered by the same hand, and Miss Paris cannot possibly have murdered George Hawken. What is your opinion, Luke?"

"I cannot for a moment believe that Francine is guilty," said Luke. "You will remember that on Wednesday afternoon she came here and asked to speak to me in private. She is never emotional, and on this occasion she was perfectly calm and collected. She told me that, although Dr. Kent had said nothing to her, her nursing experience made her doubt that Sir Matthew had suddenly died a natural death.

"I asked her if she believed that he had been poisoned. She replied that though she did not actually believe that, she could not reject the possibility. I asked her to tell me the truth. Had she had any hand in causing the death of Sir Matthew? She declared solemnly that she had not, and I believed her."

"She did not seem offended at being asked that question?" Merrion asked.

"Not in the least," Luke replied. "She said that if it turned out that in fact Sir Matthew had been poisoned, everyone would suspect her, since she had had the best opportunity of anyone of poisoning him."

"I see no reason why the secret should not be kept, at least for the present," said Merrion. "Sooner or later, Mr. Bridgwater will have to be told, of course. As for Arnold, I feel inclined to let him find it out for himself. By withholding it from him, we should not be impeding the course of justice."

"Are you sure of that?" Luke asked.

"Quite sure," Merrion replied. "Take the logical point of view. The fact that you have told me certainly makes Miss Paris liable to suspicion. But it is far from being proof of her guilt. By concealing that fact, we are not hindering Arnold in any way."

"I'll be guided by you," said Luke. "And now I see Mrs. Welback coming to tell us that tea is ready."

They went into the drawing-room, where they found Mavis sitting at the tea table. "Well, have you two made up your minds as to who poisoned Sir Matthew?" she asked."

"We're leaving that to Arnold," her husband replied "What is your opinion?"

"I know very well what Mrs. Aintree's opinion will be," said Mavis. "But I don't share it. If Miss Paris had been guilty, she couldn't have given her evidence as frankly and straightforwardly as she did."

"I'm inclined to agree with you there," Merrion replied. "I wonder if she made the same impression on Arnold as she did on you. Ah, there he is."

"Come in and have your tea, Mr. Arnold," said Luke as Arnold entered the room. "Have you anything fresh to tell us?"

"Quite a lot," Arnold replied. He repeated the conversations he had had since the inquest. "Charlie's yarn sounds utterly incredible," he went on. "Particularly that part about the coloured man who gave him a bottle of whisky. Wherever that bottle came from, it wasn't sent to Charlie by Sir Matthew. But the missing smock and apron have been found. On our way here Filland and I met Jarrow, and he told us.

"It seems that soon after we left Jarrow in the village, he saw two small boys prancing along the street. One was wearing a smock and the other an apron. Jarrow recognised these as Charlie's property. He stopped the boys and asked them where they had got the things. They told him that they had found them lying in a dry ditch about a quarter of a mile along the Dersham road. Jarrow confiscated them and took them to Charlie, who identified them as his property. Jarrow asked him if he had thrown them away in the ditch. To which Charlie replied indignantly that he certainly hadn't. They were far too useful to him for him to have done a thing like that."

"There appears to be a grain of truth in Charlie's yarn," Merrion remarked.

"There may be," Arnold replied. "I'm not worrying my head about it, because it is of no importance. What is of importance are the two facts I learnt from Albert Oakley. The first concerns Charlie. While Albert had gone down to see who was in the car that had driven up, Charlie brought in some roses and took them to the studio. Since Miss Paris was not there to take them,

Sir Matthew told Charlie to put them on the table by the bed. And that was the table on which lay the box of tablets.

"The second fact concerns the visitor whom Sir Matthew received. After his dismissal, this visitor was alone in the studio. Not for more than a few seconds. But that would have given him time to slip a tablet of potassium cyanide into the box. If he had put it on the top of the tablets already there, it would have been the first to come to Miss Paris's fingers. She told me that she had merely picked out a tablet, without looking at it very carefully."

"So we have two more people who had the opportunity," said Merrion. "Does it seem very likely that Charlie slipped a poisonous tablet into the box?"

"No, it doesn't," Arnold replied. "Though he could have got the potassium cyanide easily enough from any chemist, say in Dersham. He had only to say that he wanted it to put in a wasps' nest. But he must have known well enough that he had nothing to gain by Sir Matthew's death."

"Are you inclined to suspect the sombrely clad visitor?" Merrion asked.

"If I'm right in believing him to have been Green, the art dealer, I am," Arnold replied. "Your imagination has already suggested a motive for him. In any case, I shall make it my business to interview Green when I get back to London."

"Quite right," said Merrion. "But, while you're still here, it might pay you to look a little more closely. What did really happen to Charlie that day? He had come by a bottle of whisky which he could not have bought locally. If he had stolen it, it doesn't seem likely that he would have mentioned it at all. It is possible that he is telling the truth, and the bottle was given to him.'

"You don't believe his yarn about the coloured man, surely?" Arnold asked.

Merrion smiled. "Not implicitly. But he may have had a visitor who had blackened his hands and face as a means of disguise."

"But why should anyone have made Charlie a present of a bottle of whisky?" Arnold asked. "For obvious reasons," Merrion replied. "The donor who must have been aware of Charlie's failing, knew what would happen. And happen it did. Charlie wasted no time in getting down to the whisky, and kept at it till he was completely sozzled. The man who had given him the bottle allowed what he considered a suitable time to elapse. Then he went back to the cottage to find, as he had expected, Charlie fast asleep and snoring. This gave him the opportunity of taking the smock and apron which, on his first visit, he had seen hanging up to dry."

"But what did he want with the things?" Arnold demanded. "They certainly can't be worth the price of a bottle of whisky."

"I'll answer your question by another," Merrion replied. "Who was it that Miss Paris saw coming over the drawbridge as she left the house that afternoon?"

"Charlie," said Arnold. "She knew him by the smock and apron that he was wearing. Which blows your precious theory sky high."

Merrion shook his head. "I think not. Miss Paris recognised the smock and apron. But it may not have been Charlie who was wearing them."

"I don't see what you're driving at, Desmond," said Luke. "Why should anyone want to rig himself up in Charlie's kit?"

"In order to gain admission to Moat Barn," Merrion replied. "A visitor arriving without an appointment would have been turned away. But Charlie seems to have been allowed to come and go as he pleased. My man can't have known that he would find the drawbridge already down."

"Well, even if you're right, what about it?" Arnold asked. "Your man, as you call him, can't have been responsible for the death of Sir Matthew. He was already dead when Miss Paris saw the man she supposed to be Charlie."

"It is not impossible that this man had been on the premises earlier in the day," Merrion replied. "He returned there in the afternoon to learn how matters stood. I think you should try to discover what became of him. He probably made his way to Dersham, throwing Charlie's belongings into the ditch as he went."

"I'll have a word with Filland," said Arnold. "I'm looking to you to drive me into Dersham, because I want to get back to London."

Chapter X

On arriving at Scotland. Yard, Arnold consulted the telephone directory. There were dozens of Greens, but one entry seemed promising. "Green Galleries, 19 Scole Street, W.I." It was too late that evening to make a call, since the galleries would probably be closed. But on Saturday morning Arnold set out for Scole Street.

Number 19 had a shop window, displaying various pictures. Arnold went in, to find a girl seated at a desk. He showed her his card, and asked if he might speak to Mr. Green. The girl took the card into an inner office and returned to tell Arnold that Mr. Green would see him.

She showed him into the office, where a short man dressed in black was seated at a table strewn with art publications. He rose as Arnold came in.

"Sit down, Mr. Arnold," he said. "To what do I owe the distinction of a visit from the police?"

"I am making certain inquiries," Arnold replied. "I believe that one day in May you called upon Mr. George Hawken, at Cliff Cottage, Port Bosun?"

"That is correct," Green replied. "I will tell you why I went to see Mr. Hawken. One of my customers told me that he would like to acquire one of his paintings. Long ago he had seen some of his work and had been much struck by it, but at that time had not been in a position to buy any of it. Now he was prepared to buy one of his pictures and to pay a good price for it. I knew where Mr. Hawken lived, for some years ago I was in correspondence with him. I drove down to Port Bosun and had an interview with him in his studio. He showed me his pictures, and I chose two of them. I brought them back here, and the next time my customer called, I showed them to him. He chose one of them and took it away. The other is hanging in the gallery, awaiting a purchaser."

"You paid Mr. Hawken in cash for the pictures, I believe," Arnold asked.

"That is so," Green replied. "I paid him in notes on the spot, as is always my practice in dealing with artists."

"You are aware that Mr. Hawken was killed in the course of the following month?" Arnold asked.

"No, I was not aware of it," Green replied. "And I am very sorry to hear it. I cannot claim to have been an intimate friend of Mr. Hawken, but on the comparatively rare occasions that we met, he and I always got on very well together."

"Now we come to another thing," said Arnold. "On Wednesday last you called on Sir Matthew Hawken at Moat Barn?"

Green nodded. "I did. And I was profoundly shocked to see the notice of his death in yesterday's newspaper."

"I am told that your conversation with Sir Matthew ended in disagreement?" Arnold suggested.

"I am sorry to say that it did," Green replied. "I suppose it was my fault, though my intentions were of the best. I thought I could do Sir Matthew a good turn, but he wouldn't have it."

"Will you tell me what your conversation with Sir Matthew was about?" Arnold asked.

"Well, yes," Green replied hesitatingly. "You will understand that artists are temperamental, and require tactful handling. About a week ago I received a letter from an American friend of mine. He told me that he wanted a Sisley to add to his collection, and asked me if I could get him one.

"Now, many years ago I had sold a Sisley to Sir Matthew, and it occurred to me that he might be willing to sell it back to me, of course at a considerable profit to himself. But I didn't care to write to him making an offer. Sir Matthew was very chary about parting with a picture by another artist which he admired. But I thought that if Sir Matthew would grant me an interview, I might be able to persuade him to the deal.

"But, as I knew very well that if I descended upon Sir Matthew without warning he would refuse to see me, I had to contrive some pretext for an interview. After thinking over this for some time, I had an idea. I would suggest to Sir Matthew that it might be possible for me to arrange a retrospective show of his work, and ask for an appointment to discuss the matter with him. I wrote to that effect, and in return received one of Sir Matthew's cards, on which was written 'Wednesday, 12th July, morning.'

"I drove down to Moat Barn that morning. I had never been there before, and was amazed to find that the place was like a medieval castle, complete with moat and drawbridge. The drawbridge was up, and I was wondering how I was to get in when a man lowered it. He asked me if I had an appointment, and I showed him the card, which seemed to satisfy him."

"What reason had you for not telling the man your name?" Arnold asked.

"Just this," Green replied. "I thought it quite possible that Sir Matthew might not want his staff to know who his visitor was. The man took me up to the house and showed me into the studio, where I found Sir Matthew. He seemed interested in the suggestion which I had made to him and asked me how I proposed to set about it. I replied that the suggestion had been merely tentative. If he agreed to it, the preparations would obviously take some time. We discussed the matter, and Sir Matthew showed me the pictures hanging in the studio, and told me which of them he would like exhibited. Among his own pictures, I saw the Sisley which I had sold him.

"As tactfully as I could, I turned the subject to this, and asked Sir Matthew if he would care to sell it back to me, mentioning a price which I thought would tempt him. He immediately became suspicious, and curtly refused my offer. I told him I might raise the price by a few guineas, but he had become suspicious. He asked me if my true reason for seeking an interview was to try to buy the Sisley. I confessed that I had hoped that he would sell it to me, and with that he turned on me. He told me that I had gained admission to Moat Barn under false pretences, and that I was not to attempt to enter the premises again. He wheeled himself off indignantly into another room, leaving me standing. In a minute or so the man who had let me in appeared, and led me down to my car."

"What did you do during that minute or so?" Arnold asked.

A guilty expression came into Green's eyes. "There wasn't very much that I could do," he replied.

"Did you touch anything on the table standing by Sir Matthew's bed?" Arnold asked.

"Certainly not," Green replied. "I saw the bed, of course, but I don't remember noticing a table standing beside it."

"Listen to me, Mr. Green," said Arnold sternly. "Your

manner assures me that you have not told me the whole truth. Before we go any further, I must warn you that anything you say may be used in evidence. Within an hour after you left Moat Barn Sir Matthew died of poisoning. Can you offer any explanation of that?"

"No, I can't," Green replied desperately. "I didn't poison him, if that's what you think."

"How can you convince me of that?" Arnold asked. "I suggest that while you were alone in the studio you put a poisonous tablet in the box which you found on the table."

"I did nothing of the kind!" Green exclaimed. "Why should I have wanted to poison Sir Matthew?"

"For this reason," said Arnold. "You expected that upon Sir Matthew's death his collection of pictures would be sold. You would then be able to acquire what you wanted."

"But it's ridiculous," Green replied. "Where could I have got the poisonous tablet?"

"You brought it with you," said Arnold. "Just in case Sir Matthew should refuse your offer to buy the Sisley. Now, be reasonable, Mr. Green. You have not told me the whole truth. Unless you do so, I shall be bound to ask you to accompany me to Scotland Yard, where you will be charged with the murder of Sir Matthew. What exactly did you do while you were alone in the studio at Moat Barn?"

This threat had the effect which Arnold had expected. Green's resistance, never very strong, broke down completely.

"I didn't try to poison Sir Matthew," he replied. I'm not a murderer, but I'll confess now to being a thief. The Sisley was quite a small picture, hanging in an inconspicuous place. I took it down and put it in the pocket of my raincoat."

"But sooner or later Sir Matthew would have missed it?" Arnold asked.

"I hoped it would be later," Green replied. "My intention was this. As soon as my friend had bought the picture, I would send Sir Matthew the sum I had offered him. He would have been furious, but I did not believe that he would take legal action."

"Your friend would be unaware that he was acting as a receiver of stolen property," said Arnold sternly. "Where is the picture now?"

"Hanging in the gallery, awaiting inspection by my friend,"

Green replied. "He is coming here on Monday in order to do so."

"I'm afraid that your friend will be disappointed,' said Arnold dryly. "I must ask you to hand the picture over to me now. The police will keep it in safe custody until it can be returned to its rightful owners."

"Who are its rightful owners, Mr. Arnold?" Green asked eagerly.

"It seems that Sir Matthew died intestate," Arnold replied. "That being so, his two nephews will inherit his estate. You may be able to persuade them to sell you the picture. I don't know. Now will you let me have it without further delay?"

"I suppose I must," said Green. "Will you come into the gallery?" He opened an inner door, and they passed into the gallery, which was hung with picture of every description. Among them was a small one which Green pointed out. "That is the one. Small though it is, it is worth a lot of money. Will you take the greatest care of it?"

Arnold smiled. "The police are not apt to be careless about such matters. But how am I to know that this is the picture which you stole from the studio at Moat Barn?"

Green shrugged his shoulders. "You'll have to take my word for it, Mr. Arnold. Since I have confessed to the theft, I am not likely to try to double cross you now." He took down the picture and handed it to Arnold. "Shall I be prosecuted for this?" he asked nervously.

"That rests with the owners of the picture," Arnold replied. "Have you any other stolen property that you would like to surrender?"

"Certainly not!" Green exclaimed. "I have never done such a thing before, and I shall never do it again. The temptation to take it was too great, and I acted on the spur of the moment. It is perfectly true that I intended to pay Sir Matthew for it."

Arnold left Scole Street carrying the picture. He hailed a taxi and drove back to Scotland Yard. Having deposited the picture in a safe, he sent for Detective-Sergeant Wighton who duly appeared.

"I've got a job for you, Sergeant," said Arnold. "Get along to Rutland House in the City. Contact the porters, and ask them if they saw Mr. Hubert Benson about the place on Wednesday. When you've found out all you can, come back and report to me."

Wighton had not been gone many minutes when Arnold was called on the telephone by the sergeant on duty. "There's a man here who gives his name as Barry Benson, sir," said the sergeant. "He says he has some information for the police. Will you see him, sir?"

"Indeed I will," Arnold replied. "Send him up to me at once."

In a few minutes a constable escorted Barry into the room. He was a sorry figure, wearing a ragged suit and a dirty cloth cap. Arnold pointed to a chair. "Sit down. Your name is Barry Benson?"

"That's right," Barry replied. "I haven't got a visiting card, but I can show you my driving licence if you like."

He produced the licence from his pocket and handed it to Arnold. It had been issued by the London County Council to Barry Benson, with an address in Stepney. "Where were you on Wednesday, 14th June?" Arnold asked as he handed back the licence.

"In Thramsbury," Barry replied. "I had driven a van with a load of bacon down from London."

"Just so," said Arnold. "But you did not stay in Thramsbury all day. Before you answer the questions which I am going to ask you I must warn you that anything you say may be used in evidence. You went to Port Bosun, and got there a little before nine o'clock, did you not?"

Barry shook his head. "No, I didn't. I didn't go there until the middle of the day, after I had spoken to Mr. Saxthorpe."

"Are you quite sure of that?" Arnold asked. "You arrived at Thramsbury at about half-past seven. You were not seen there again until about noon. How did you spend the morning?"

"I'd been driving all night," Barry replied. "After I had reported at Mr. Saxthorpe's place, I went and got some breakfast at a cafe. Then I went back to the rest-room and had a nap. When I woke up, I went to see Mr. Saxthorpe to get my orders for the return load. He told me that I couldn't get loaded up until the evening, and that I was to drive to Juniper Farm at six o'clock."

"You offered to drive the van to Thramsbury in order to have the opportunity of visiting Port Bosun?" Arnold asked.

"Well, yes, I did," Barry replied. "I was nearly as broke then as I am now, and I knew that if I could see my Uncle George he would help me out."

"What steps did you take to see your uncle?" Arnold asked.

"After Mr. Saxthorpe had told me that I shouldn't be wanted until six o'clock, I took a bus to Port Bosun," Barry replied. "I felt sure that I should find Uncle George at home at lunch-time. When I got off the bus I walked to Cliff Cottage and hammered on the door. There was no reply, but the door was not locked and I went in. There was no sign of Uncle George, but his shooting-stick was not in its usual place, so I guessed that he was out sketching. I waited for half an hour or so, and then it dawned upon me that Uncle George might have taken his lunch with him, in which case he would probably not be back until the later afternoon."

"You didn't go and look for your uncle?" Arnold asked.

"What would have been the good of that?" Barry replied. "He might have been anywhere. I didn't know where to start looking for him. But I saw that I had another opportunity of seeing him. He would be sure to come home when the light became too bad for sketching."

"What was that opportunity?" Arnold asked. "Just this," Barry replied. "When the van had been loaded at Juniper Farm, I could come back by the direct road from Westhaven to Port Bosun, which passes Cliff Cottage. I could hop out and see Uncle George who would surely be at home by that time."

"What did you do while you were waiting in Cliff Cottage, expecting your uncle to come home?" Arnold asked.

Barry shifted uneasily in his chair. "I don't know that I did anything particular. I just hung about."

"Now, look here, Benson," said Arnold sternly. "If you expect me to believe what you tell me, you must tell the complete truth. The police know what you did while you were at Cliff Cottage. You may as well confess."

"Oh, very well," Barry replied after some hesitation. "You'll remember that I came here of my own free will. That ought to be a point in my favour. It struck me that, after all, I might not find Uncle George on my way back from Juniper Farm. He might have gone away for a day or two, as he sometimes did.

"But I knew where he kept his money. In a biscuit tin under a settee in the studio. I found the tin there and opened it. To my surprise there was a lot of money in it. Four packets of pound-notes, each held together by a rubber band, besides some loose notes and silver. The sight of so much money was a temptation I couldn't resist. I took three of the packets of notes and stuffed them into my pocket."

"To put it bluntly, you stole your uncle's money," Arnold remarked.

"It wasn't really stealing," Barry protested. "If I had seen Uncle George that evening, I should have told him what I had done, and asked him if I could keep the money until I could pay him back. Of course, when I took the notes, I didn't know that I should never see him again."

"Well, go on with your story," said Arnold. "What did you do after you had taken the notes?"

"I took the bus back to Thramsbury," Barry replied. "I had some food at the cafe and then, since I had nothing to do till six o'clock, I wandered round the town for a bit. Soon after five I went back to the cafe for a cup of tea. I meant to stay there until it was time for me to pick up the van."

"Why didn't you go back to the van?" Arnold asked.

"I didn't dare to," Barry replied. "I was just thinking of leaving the cafe when a couple of chaps from Port Bosun came in. They sat down at the table next to mine. I knew them by sight, but I didn't know their names, and they didn't seem to recognise me. And then I heard one of them mention the name of Mr. Hawken.

"Naturally I listened to what they were talking about. To my horror I heard that Uncle George had been found dead on the rocks not far from Cliff | Cottage. He appeared to have fallen from the cliff above, and the two men seemed to be agreed that he lust have been pushed over.

"You can imagine my feelings. It was known that I had been in Port Bosun that day, and I must have been seen walking towards Cliff Cottage. I had Uncle George's money in my pocket, and it would be said that I had murdered him in order to get it, and I couldn't prove that I hadn't. I didn't dare show myself. I was in a state of panic, and I felt that I must hide myself until the affair had blown over."

"You would have done far better to go to the police then and told them your story," said Arnold. "Your uncle is believed to have been killed about nine o'clock that morning. Where were you at that time?"

"In the rest-room at Mr. Saxthorpe's place," Barry replied. "But, so far as I know, no one came in and saw me there."

"Which is unfortunate," said Arnold. "Where did you go when you left the cafe?"

"To the railway station, where I took a train to Bristol," Barry replied. "I had been there before, with a lorry, because it was one of my regular runs when I was with Aspalls. I put up for the night at a place that I knew of, but where I wasn't known. Then in the morning I walked along the quays, without any clear idea of what I meant to do.

"Then tied up alongside I saw a small Irish ship. She was loading, and an idea came to me. I asked one of the chaps on the quay where she was bound for, and he told me she was sailing for Dublin that evening. I went on board, found the skipper, and asked him if he would give me a passage to Dublin if I paid him for it.

"He said he couldn't do that, because his ship wasn't licensed to carry passengers. But he said that he was short of a deckhand, who had fallen into one of the holds and been taken to hospital. If I cared to sign on in his place, he would take me to Dublin, and it would cost me nothing.

"Naturally, I fell in with that at once. He took me to an office, where I signed on. Not in my own name, but as Billy Bawtry. Then I went back to the ship, where I laid low until sailing time. We got to Dublin next day. I said good-bye to the skipper and went ashore. But I didn't stay in Dublin. I took a train to the west coast, where I felt pretty sure that I should never be found."

"That is a most extraordinary story," said Arnold. "But, before you go any further, tell me this. You said just now that it was known that you had been in Port Bosun that Wednesday. What did you mean by that? Who knew that you had been to Port Bosun?"

"I'll tell you," Barry replied. "When I got off the bus there, one of the Penwarnes was standing on the pavement. Mark, the third brother. He and I had chummed up when I had been staying with Uncle George, and of course he recognised me at once. We had a short chat, and he said that he supposed that

I was on my way to see my uncle. I told him that I was, and left him there."

"I see," said Arnold. "Now we'll get back to the story of your adventures. You went to the west coast of Ireland. What brought you back to England?"

"Sheer necessity," Barry replied. "I thought that I should be able to get a job of some kind, but I found that there were no jobs going. I might have found a driving job, but I didn't dare apply for one, because the name on my driving licence would have given me away. I'm bound to say that the chaps I met weren't inquisitive. I think they must have guessed I was on the run, as they call it. But in those parts being on the run is almost normal.

"I had to live somehow, and that meant dipping into Uncle George's money. It wasn't very long before I had only a few pounds left, with no prospect of earning any more. I was almost at my wits' end. I knew that Uncle George had left me Cliff Cottage in his will, and that Mr. Clapdale and I were the executors. But that was no use to me, because I daren't come out into the open. At last I came to the conclusion that the only thing I could do was to throw myself on the mercy of my Uncle Matthew. I knew that was a forlorn hope, because the last time I had been to Moat Barn he had refused to see me. But there was nothing else to be done, and I decided to try my luck."

"When did you come back to England?" Arnold asked.

"Last Monday," Barry replied. "I had learnt how easy it was to slip across the border into Northern Ireland. So I left the village where I had been staying, and tramped my way to Belfast. I still had enough money for what I meant to do, and from there I took a steerage passage to Liverpool. Then, with almost the last of my remaining money I bought a ticket to London.

"I didn't venture into my old haunts in Stepney, where I should have run too great a risk of being recognised. I found a room in the Borough, and sat down to consider what I should do next. I began to see that any attempt to penetrate the defences of Moat Barn was doomed to failure. Uncle Matthew would refuse to see me, as he had on the last occasion. The drawbridge would be up against me, and Albert would be forbidden to lower it.

"But what else could I do? It would be hopeless to appeal to Hubert. He was far too stingy to help me. Besides, he probably believed that I had murdered Uncle George, and it was quite likely that he would hand me over to the police. I couldn't go down to Port Bosun and claim my inheritance from Mr. Clapdale. That would indeed be putting my head in the lion's mouth. Then, on Wednesday morning, I had a wild idea. I saw how it might be possible for me to gain access to Moat Barn. Once there, I would force myself upon Uncle Matthew and beg him to listen to me."

Chapter XI

The odd adventure of Charlie Potter at once became clear to Arnold. But it would be better to allow Barry to explain matters for himself. "You went to Moat Barn on Wednesday morning?" Arnold asked.

"I only got as far as Shepherd Green in the morning," Barry replied. "I had just enough money left to buy a bottle of whisky and a packet of ground charcoal. I set off on foot, but I hadn't got far out of London when a lorry driver pulled up and asked me if I wanted a lift. I told him that I was a lorry driver myself, and that it was my day off and that I wanted to get to Shepherd Green. He said that he wasn't going as far as that, only to Dersham. If I wanted a lift as far as that, I was welcome. That was a stroke of luck, and naturally I accepted the offer.

"When the lorry reached Dersham, I got out and set off on foot again. As it was raining, I thought that Charlie Potter wouldn't be out at work, so I made for his cottage. Just before I got there I rubbed the ground charcoal over my face and hands. I wasn't sure that Charlie wouldn't recognise me, unless I adopted some sort of disguise, and I thought that a simple blackening would be good enough.

"Sure enough Charlie was sitting in his kitchen, with the door wide open. I gave him the bottle of whisky, and told him that I had come from Moat Barn, and that Sir Matthew had asked me to take the whisky to Charlie. It was a most impossible yarn, but I knew that Charlie, once in possession of a bottle of whisky, wouldn't ask too many questions as to where it came from.

"I hid up for the next three or four hours, until I reckoned that the whisky would have had time to produce its effect. By then the rain had washed the black off my face and hands. I went back to the cottage to find Charlie fast asleep and snoring. On my first visit I had seen his smock and apron hanging up to dry. They were still there, and I put them on. Then I started off for Moat Barn.

"I had made up my mind exactly what I meant to do. Seeing

a man whom he would suppose to be Charlie, Albert would come down and lower the drawbridge for him. Of course when we came face to face he would have seen that it wasn't Charlie at all. But I didn't mean to let him obstruct me. I should have pushed him aside, or into the moat if he proved troublesome. He wouldn't have drowned, for the water isn't deep enough. But it would have taken him some little time for him to climb out and come after me. And by then I hoped to be with Uncle Matthew.

"But things didn't turn out as I had expected. When I got to Moat Barn I saw that the drawbridge was down, and that there was no obstacle in my way. I started up the path, but before I had gone more than a few yards, I saw Francine leaving the house. I turned off into the garden, so as not to meet her. It seemed that luck was on my side. With Francine out of the way, there would be no one to prevent me from reaching Uncle Matthew. Except Albert, who would probably be in the kitchen. If it had been fine, Uncle Matthew would probably have been out on the terrace. But since it was wet, he would certainly be in the studio.

"I came out of the garden and went to the front door, which I knew would not be locked. I opened it and went into the studio. I had expected to find Uncle Matthew in his chair, but he wasn't. The empty chair was drawn up by the bedside, and the door between the studio and the kitchen was shut.

"I couldn't understand it. If Uncle Matthew had decided to spend the afternoon in bed, Francine would hardly have gone out. Or, if it had been absolutely necessary for her to do so, she would have left the kitchen door open, so that Albert would be within call. Very quietly I went up to the bed. It was an old-fashioned four-poster, with curtains which were drawn.

"I drew them back and peeped in. Uncle Matthew was lying there, and at first I thought that he was asleep. But I very soon found that he was not breathing, and the ghastly truth dawned upon me that he was dead.

"What was I to do now? I must not be found at Moat Barn, rigged up in Charlie's togs. I crept out of the house and hurried along towards the village, dreading every minute that I should meet Francine on her way back. I didn't, and I got through the village without seeing anyone I knew. Then I set off towards Dersham. When I was some little way out of the village, I took off

Charlie's smock and apron and threw them into the ditch. I felt that I had compensated Charlie for his old rags by giving him a bottle of whisky."

"Charlie didn't quite see it in that light," said Arnold. "You told him that you had been to Moat Barn that morning. Was that the truth?"

"No, it wasn't," Barry replied. "I shouldn't have ventured there until I had disguised myself as Charlie. That was the whole idea."

"What did you do next?" Arnold asked.

"I felt that I must hang around until I knew how Uncle Matthew had died," Barry replied. "I still had a few shillings left, and I walked back to Dersham and found a room there, still in the name of Billy Bawtry, of course. Next day I found that everyone was talking about Uncle Matthew. Very few of the Dersham folk had ever seen him, but he had become something of a legendary figure. It was known that he had at one time been a distinguished artist, and people wondered why he had shut himself up in Moat Barn with a woman young enough to be his granddaughter. The general opinion seemed to be that Francine had got tired of him and had put him to sleep in order to inherit his money. I learnt that there was to be an inquest, and I decided to stay where I was until I had heard the verdict."

"And you did hear it, I take it?" Arnold asked.

"I heard it on Friday evening," Barry replied. "And I was horrified to learn that Uncle Matthew had been poisoned. I can't believe that Francine poisoned him. She always seemed to be devoted to him."

"Who else, then?" Arnold asked. "Now tell me the truth, Benson. You had been to Moat Barn that Wednesday morning. And while you were there, you had put a poisonous tablet in the box on your uncle's bedside table."

"But that's ridiculous!" Barry exclaimed. "In the first place, I didn't go to Moat Barn in the morning. I hadn't got hold of Charlie's togs by then. And why on earth should I have wanted to poison Uncle Matthew, who was my only hope? I don't for a moment suppose that he had left me anything in his will."

"Very well," said Arnold. "Now tell me why you came here this morning?"

"To tell the truth," Barry replied, "I was tired of being on the run, and I knew that the police must find me sooner or later. I had no money left, and I didn't know where to look for any. It seemed to me that the only thing I could do was to give myself up and take the consequences. I tramped up from Dersham last night."

"The consequences are that you will be detained pending inquiries into the truth of your statements," said Arnold. "If necessary, you will be charged with the theft of Mr. George Hawken's money."

"I'm only too glad to be detained," Barry replied. "Because I suppose I shall be fed, and that is all I want. I haven't had a meal since yesterday morning."

"We'll see to that," said Arnold. "Take him away, Constable, and give him something to eat."

The constable marched Barry from the room, leaving Arnold to consider the remarkable story he had heard. How far was Barry to be believed? Had he in fact murdered either or both of his uncles?

Arnold decided to start with the case of Mr. George Hawken. He put a call through to Superintendent Egford at Thramsbury, and very soon heard his voice on the telephone.

"Why, Mr. Arnold, its a long time since I heard anything from you. Have you any news for me?"

"I've got Barry Benson on the premises here," Arnold replied.

"The dickens you have!" Egford exclaimed. "Has he confessed to having murdered his uncle?"

"He denies that he did," Arnold replied. "I'll come down and tell you his story. But first of all, I should like to know whether the Penwarnes are likely to be on shore to-morrow."

"I'll ring up Docking at Port Bosun," said Egford. "When I've heard what he has to say about that, I'll ring you back."

Arnold turned to other matters. Half an hour later his telephone rang, and he was told that Superintendent Egford was on the line. He asked that he should be put through, and heard Egford's voice again.

"Is that you, Mr. Arnold? I've had Docking's report. He says that all four Penwarnes are out in Seabird, but that they are expected to come into port on this afternoon's tide. They never go out on Sundays, so they are sure to be at home to-morrow."

"Then I'll come down by the night train as usual," Arnold replied. "If you can make it convenient to meet me, I'll tell you why I'm interested in the Penwarnes."

Soon after this conversation had ended, Wighton appeared.

"I've been to Rutland House and talked to two of the porters, sir," he reported. "They remember Wednesday, because it was the first wet day for two or three weeks. I spoke to them separately, and they both gave me the same information. Mr. Benson reached his office at half-past nine, and was there all the morning. He didn't go out to lunch until half-past one, and was out for less than an hour. He was back in his office before half-past two, and didn't leave again until nearly six."

"Good enough, Sergeant," said Arnold. "We've got Mr. Benson's brother here. I shan't be here to-morrow, but if Barry Benson says he wants to make a further statement, you can listen to what he has to say."

Egford met Arnold at Thramsbury station on Sunday morning, and drove him to the Three Lions. As they had breakfast together, Arnold repeated Barry's story. "And what do you make of that?" he asked.

"It sounds crazy to me," Egford replied. "Although he denies having murdered his uncle, he admits that he took his money. What do you make of him, Mr. Arnold?"

"I hardly know," Arnold replied. "He can hardly have made up that extraordinary yarn of his. We can check up on his meeting with Mark Penwarne."

"Easily enough," Egford agreed. "We'll drive to Port Bosun and go to Docking's house. We'll tell him to bring Mark Penwarne along, and we can talk to him there."

This they did when they had finished breakfast. Docking took them into the room that he used as his office, and went off in search of Mark. In a few minutes he returned with Mark in his company. Mark was dressed in his Sunday best, a not very well-fitting blue suit and a pair of shoes which were obviously too small for him. He was dark, with a rather sullen expression and seemed ill at ease in the presence of police.

"Sit down, Penwarne," said Arnold, pointing to a chair opposite his own. "Do you remember the day on which Mr. Hawken was killed?"

"Naturally," Mark replied. "Two of my brothers went out in

the boat and brought his body in."

"You are acquainted with Mr. Hawken's nephew, Barry Benson, I believe?" Arnold asked. "When did you last see him?"

"Why, that very day," Mark replied. "It was quite by chance. This was how it came about. We had ordered a new riding light for Seabird from a shop in Plymouth. It was to be sent that Wednesday, by train to Thramsbury, and then by bus along here. We wanted it badly, because the old one had packed up and we were going out again that evening. I met every bus that day, hoping that the riding light would be on one of them. But it wasn't till the three o'clock bus that it came."

"You met every bus from Thramsbury?" Arnold asked. "Did you meet the one that arrives here at eight-forty in the morning?"

"Yes, I did," Mark replied. "That's the first that comes in."

"Did Barry Benson arrive on that bus?" Arnold asked.

Mark shook his head. "Not on that one. I couldn't have missed him if he had. He got off the bus that gets here at twelve-forty. I saw him and we had a short chat. I asked him what he was doing now, and he told me he had a job driving lorries for a London firm. He had driven a van to Thramsbury, and he hadn't to go back till that evening. I said that I supposed he had come here to see his uncle, and he told me that he had."

"You didn't see him leave here, I suppose?" Arnold asked.

"It wasn't likely that I should," Mark replied. "I didn't watch the buses that left here. Only the ones that came in."

"What is your opinion of Barry?" Arnold asked.

"He's a decent sort of chap," Mark replied. "I don't think he'd do anyone a dirty trick. His trouble is that he can never stick to anything. He gets tired of a job before he's properly started on it. He told me that among other things he'd been an actor, a shop assistant, and a courier. And he's always broke, because whenever he earns any money he gambles it away. He borrowed a couple of quid from me once, and I've never had them back."

"You know that Mr. Hawken made a will, in which he left Cliff Cottage to Barry?" Arnold asked.

Mark nodded. "Yes, Barry told me that. He told me that he could never live there, for what was he to live on? He said that he supposed he could sell it, and that's what he would do when his uncle died."

"Have you ever met Barry's brother Hubert?" Arnold asked.

"I've never met him," Mark replied. "I don't know that he ever came down here. But Barry told me about him. He said that his brother was a regular toff, with a big house and two posh cars. I asked Barry if his brother wouldn't help him when he was out of a job. Barry told me that he was far too stingy for that. Besides, he had told Barry that he ought to be man enough to keep himself. Why couldn't he find himself a good job and stick to it?"

"Which is just what Barry seems to have found it impossible to do," Arnold remarked. "Did he ever speak of his other uncle, Sir Matthew Hawken?"

"Not often," Mark replied. "He told me once that his Uncle Matthew was a queer old bird, who lived behind a drawbridge and wouldn't see people. He wasn't generous like his Uncle George, and that he had no use for either of his nephews. Barry was quite sure that his Uncle Matthew would leave him nothing in his will. He understood that most of his money would go to his brother George."

"Who died before his elder brother Sir Matthew," said Arnold. "Now tell me this. Do you know if there was any stranger in Port Bosun on the day that Mr. Hawken was killed? By stranger I mean anyone who did not live here?"

Mark's answer was hesitating. "Well, I know of one. But I can't talk about him."

"Why can't you talk about him?" Arnold asked.

"Because he made us all promise not to speak about him to anyone," Mark replied.

"That's all very well," said Arnold. "But when the police are making inquiries, that sort of promise isn't binding. I don't want to threaten you, Penwarne, but I should like you to understand this. It is an offence to impede the police in the exercise of their duty."

Mark looked thoroughly alarmed. "You mean that you could run me in if I didn't tell you what I knew?"

"Something very like it," said Arnold. "But don't let's talk like that. I'm sure you'll be reasonable and tell us who this stranger was?"

"He wasn't a stranger to us," Mark replied. "We've known

him for some years now. Though it isn't more than once in a couple of months or so that we see him."

"Who is this man, and how did you come to know him?" Arnold asked.

"Well, that's a long story," Mark replied. "It began one summer evening, some years ago, as I say. The four of us were getting Seabird ready for sea, when a gentleman came strolling along the quay. He stopped when he came up to us, and watched us for a bit. Then he asked if we were going out fishing.

"My eldest brother Jake, who is the skipper, answered him and told him that we were, as soon as the tide made. Then the gentleman asked where our fishing ground was to be. Jake told him that it was in mid-Channel, about halfway between here and the French coast.

"Then the gentleman asked if he could come with us. He would of course pay for the privilege. Jake told him that he could come if he liked, but that he would have to rough it. There was a spare bunk in the fo'c'sle, and he could have the use of that. He said that he was used to roughing it, and stepped on board.

"As soon as the tide made, we left harbour. It was nearly a flat calm, and we used the engine. Jake set the course, and Amos took the helm. As soon as we were well under way, the rest of us set to work arranging the gear, the gentleman lending a hand. After a while I cooked the supper and laid it on the cabin table. Lew, the youngest, took over the wheel from Amos and the other three of us sat down to supper with the gentleman.

"While we were having supper, the gentleman took out four five-pound notes from his wallet and laid them down before Jake, who said that was far too much to pay for a fishing trip. The gentleman replied that it was time that he explained why he had asked to come with us. He knew some French fishermen who worked from Les Baleines, a small French port, and he wanted to join them. Their boat was called the Marie Touchet, and they would be fishing fifty miles south of the Lizard at dawn. Could Jake arrange to meet the Marie Touchet?

"Jake thought this over for a bit. Then he said that twenty pounds was well worth earning, and that he thought he could manage it. It wouldn't take us very far out of our way, for where we meant to fish was more or less in that direction. He got up, gave Lew a fresh course and came back again, to ask our passenger his name.

"The gentleman replied that before he told us any more, we must each promise to keep our mouths shut. We gave our promises, and then he told us that his name was Battlesby, and that he was a secret agent working for the British Government on the Continent. It was necessary for him to come to England at intervals to post his reports. He dare not post them abroad, in case they should be opened and read. But he could not travel by any form of public transport, because it was essential that he should not be seen leaving or entering the Continent. That was why he had worked out this means of crossing the Channel.

"I think we were rather thrilled at the idea of helping a secret service man. Besides, as Jake had said, twenty pounds was well worth earning. We kept on our course, and we were fifty miles due south of the Lizard shortly before dawn. Jake stopped the engine, and we drifted for about an hour. Then a vessel hove in sight, and Mr. Battlesby told us that she was the Marie Touchet. Jake waved a torch towards her, and she came alongside.

"Before he left us, Mr. Battlesby asked Jake if he would oblige him again, on the same terms. Jake replied that he was quite ready to do that. Then Mr. Battlesby said that next time he wanted to come to England he would write to us, asking for a date and enclosing an addressed envelope for the reply. The Marie Touchet would bring him to the same place at the same time. He jumped on to the deck of the Marie Touchet, and we went on to our fishing ground."

"How long was it before you heard again from this Mr. Battlesby?" Arnold asked.

"About a couple of months," Mark replied. "A letter came for Jake with a foreign stamp on it. It had no address or signature, and was only a few words long. 'About a week from the time this reaches you?' Of course we knew who had sent the letter and what he meant. There was an addressed envelope enclosed. Jake wrote a date on a piece of paper, put it in the envelope and posted it. At dawn on the date he had given we got to the same place as before, and found the Marie Touchet waiting for us. Mr. Battlesby was on board, and when we came alongside he jumped on to our deck. We'd done our fishing and we brought him straight back here.

"But before we parted company with the Marie Touchet, he asked us when we should be coming out again. Jake told him in three days' time. Mr. Battlesby called out in French to the Marie Touchet's skipper, and told us that he had arranged with him for the next meeting. And so it came about."

"How were the three days spent?" Arnold asked.

"A day to get back here," Mark replied. "Then a day in port, and the third fishing and meeting the Marie Touchet:'

"What did Mr. Battlesby do on the day you were in port?" Arnold asked.

"He went ashore as soon as we tied up," Mark replied. "He had a suitcase with him, which he told us contained important documents. He was dressed just as we were, jersey, tarpaulins, sea-boots and cap. He came aboard again in the afternoon, saying that he had been to Thramsbury, where he had posted his documents."

"And the same thing has happened at intervals since then?" Arnold asked.

"Just the same," Mark replied. "A couple of months or so, as a rule, though sometimes the intervals were longer. But on the second or third time it happened, Mr. Battlesby said that people might notice that Seabird left port with four men on board and came back with five. So that we arranged that that shouldn't happen. The next time we went to fetch Mr. Battlesby he came on board us, and Lew boarded the Marie Touchet. Then, when we took Mr. Battlesby out again, he and Lew changed places. It was always Lew who stayed on board the Marie Touchet, because he spoke a little French, which we others didn't."

"I see," said Arnold. "Now we'll get back to the day on which Mr. Hawken was killed. Mr. Battlesby was on shore here, you tell us?"

"That's right," Mark replied. "It was just the same as always. We came in on the morning tide, about five o'clock. Mr. Battlesby went ashore when we'd had breakfast, soon after eight, carrying his suitcase. He came back in the afternoon and stayed on board until we sailed again on the next morning's tide."

"Do you think it possible that Mr. Battlesby knew Mr. Hawken?" Arnold asked.

"He may have done," Mark replied. "Though he has never told us that he knew anyone in Port Bosun but ourselves."

"Very well, Penwarne," said Arnold. "We needn't keep you any longer. You may be quite sure that we shan't repeat what you have told us."

Docking led Mark from the room and returned. "Well, Constable?" Arnold asked. "What do you think of what we've just heard? Is it possible that a stranger could land here without being noticed?"

"I think it's quite possible, sir," Docking replied. "Boats from other ports put in here to sell their fish, often enough. If a stranger dressed like a fisherman was seen about the place, it would be thought that he had come off one of them."

"So that Mr. Battlesby might have passed unnoticed," said Arnold. "It's rather more than a month since Mr. Hawken was killed, and that was the last time that Mr. Battlesby was here. Penwarne says that he comes to England about once in a couple of months, so that he should be expected again in three or four weeks."

"Shall we tell the Penwarnes to let us know when they hear from him?" Egford asked.

"I'd rather not do it that way," Arnold replied. "If they warned Mr. Battlesby that the police were on the lookout for him, he might stay on board the Marie Touchet, and not land here at all."

"Then what do you suggest?" Egford asked.

"Leave it to the constable," Arnold replied. "Let him keep his eye on Seabird. He will see her go out, and he will know that she will be back in two or three days. He will watch for her to come in, and if anyone other than the Penwarnes comes ashore from her, he can ring you up. You will know what steps to take."

Chapter XII

Arnold went back to London that evening. When he reached Scotland Yard on Monday morning, he sent for Barry, who was brought to his room under escort.

"Well, Benson?" Arnold asked. "Have you anything to add to the statement you made on Saturday?"

"Nothing," Barry replied. "I told you the whole truth, and I can't do any more."

"I've seen your friend Mark Penwarne," said Arnold. "He tells me that he saw you get off the midday bus at Port Bosun. But are you quite sure that you had not been there earlier in the day?"

"Absolutely certain," Barry replied. "If I had been, why should I have gone there again?"

"To create the impression that you did not know that your Uncle George was already dead," said Arnold. "What time did you leave the cafe in Thramsbury where you had breakfast?"

"It can't have been long after eight," Barry replied. "I didn't sit long over my breakfast, because I wanted to get to the rest-room and have a doss down."

"Did you go straight from the cafe to the rest-room?" Arnold asked.

"Yes, I did," Barry replied. "But I didn't see any of the chaps as I crossed the yard."

"Was your van standing there?" Arnold asked.

"Not then it wasn't," Barry replied. "One of Mr. Saxthorpe's men must have taken it away to be unloaded. But it was back again when I spoke to Mr. Saxthorpe about noon."

From Barry's manner Arnold got the impression that he was telling the truth. "Did Mark Penwarne ever speak to you about a man of the name of Battlesby?" he asked.

Barry shook his head. "He never mentioned that name. And I can't remember hearing it at any time that I was in Port Bosun."

"That will do now," said Arnold. "I think you will be best where you are for the present."

"I don't mind," Barry replied cheerfully. "I've nowhere else to go."

At a sign from Arnold the escorting constable led Barry away, and Arnold turned to the papers lying on his desk. That afternoon he put a call through to Merrion's rooms in St. James's. He thought it possible that the Merrions had left Shepherd Green and stopped in London on their way to High Eldersham.

He was right, for in a minute or two he was told that Mr. Merrion was on the line. "I thought there was just a chance of catching you," said Arnold. "How long do you propose to stay in London?"

"For two or three days," Merrion replied. "Mavis wants to see some friends and do some shopping."

"Then when would it be convenient for me to come and see you?" Arnold asked.

"Come and have dinner with me this evening," Merrion replied. "I shall be alone, because Mavis is dining with some friends."

Arnold gratefully accepted the invitation. He reached Merrion's rooms at half-past seven, and found his host expecting him.

"Well, my friend, I am very glad to see you," said Merrion as he poured out two glasses of sherry. "I dare say you've got something to tell me. We left Shepherd Green this morning. Sir Matthew was to be buried this afternoon."

"I've quite a lot to tell you," Arnold replied. He described the course of his investigations since he and Merrion had last met.

"We'll begin with Green," he went on. "He struck me as being rather a nervous sort of chap, and I felt pretty sure from his manner that he'd been up to something. When I told him that I suspected him of poisoning Sir Matthew he crumpled up. He had been up to something, not murder, but theft. He had stolen a valuable picture from Sir Matthew's collection. Of course he protested that it wasn't really theft. As soon as he had sold the picture, he meant to send Sir Matthew the price he had offered him for it. That may or may not be true. Anyhow, I took the picture and locked it up."

Merrion smiled. "How do you know that that picture came from Sir Matthew's collection? Green may have palmed off something quite worthless on you."

"I've thought of that," Arnold replied. "My own opinion is that Green was too scared to play a trick like that. However, I shall take the picture down to Moat Barn and show it to Miss Paris. If it came from the studio there, she is sure to recognise it."

"Yes," Merrion agreed. "Has it occurred to you that Green might have poisoned Sir Matthew so that the picture he had stolen should not be missed?"

"It has occurred to me," Arnold replied. "But somehow I don't see him taking a poisonous tablet to Moat Barn with him in case it should be wanted. He is obviously not above playing a mean trick, but I don't think he's a murderer."

"Well, you've talked to him and I haven't," said Merrion. "In any case, it doesn't seem likely that he murdered George Hawken. You may think that I've got a bee in my bonnet about that, but I feel certain that whoever murdered one brother murdered the other. Who comes next on your list of suspects?"

"Hubert Benson," Arnold replied. "But he's written off. I am quite satisfied that he did not leave London last Wednesday. And as he was in France at the time, he cannot have pushed brother George over the cliff. So we come to Barry.

"I've told you of my conversation with Mark Penwarne. He states very definitely that Barry did not arrive at Port Bosun by the first bus from Thramsbury. If he had set out on foot as soon as he arrived at Thramsbury, he could not have got to Port Bosun by nine o'clock. He may of course have been given a lift. I have asked Egford to make inquiries locally as to whether anyone gave a lift that morning to a man answering Barry's description. Until I have heard the result of those inquiries, I am keeping an open mind.

"But, if Barry did murder his Uncle George, there are two rather puzzling questions to be answered. Why did he go back to Port Bosun later in the day, thus advertising his presence in the neighbourhood? And again, if he overheard in the cafe that his uncle's body had been found, why should that have surprised him? He would have known that it must be found sooner or later. Why didn't he bolt earlier than he did?"

"What impression did Barry make on you while he was telling his story?" Merrion asked.

"Quite a favourable one," Arnold replied. "He seemed to have made up his mind to tell the truth, and was telling it. He's a graceless young vagabond, but I don't think he's a desperate criminal, even though he admits having stolen his uncle's money. Of course he says that he meant to pay it back. But what hope he could ever have cherished of being able to do that I don't know."

"He also admits that he was in Shepherd Green last Wednesday," Merrion remarked.

"He does," Arnold replied. "He admits that he was in the studio at Moat Barn that afternoon. But he declares that he was not there in the morning. And I'm inclined to believe him, because I don't see how he could have been. How could he have got on to the premises unless Albert had lowered the drawbridge for him? Even if he had managed to cross the moat somehow, he would have been seen as soon as he entered the house. Albert was there all the morning, and Charlie Potter for part of it. After Miss Paris had gone out, Green came along. Sir Matthew can hardly have been left alone for a moment.

"Even if Barry had caught Sir Matthew alone, he would hardly have ventured to slip a poisonous tablet into the box under his very eyes. Again if Barry had been to Moat Barn in the morning, why should he have gone back there in the afternoon, wearing Charlie's smock and apron? Merely to see whether his dodge had been successful? That doesn't seem to me at all likely."

"Perhaps not," said Merrion. "All the same, doesn't it seem rather significant that Barry was at Port Bosun on the day that his Uncle George died, and at Shepherd Green on the day when his Uncle Matthew died?"

"I'm not denying that," Arnold replied. "But, as I've tried to point out, he doesn't seem to have been in either place at the right time. I'm going to hold him for the present, until I see how things turn out. For the present, I haven't sufficient evidence to charge him with either murder. Now let's put Barry aside for the moment and turn to this most mysterious Mr. Battlesby. What do you make of him?"

"I'll tell you this," said Merrion. "I don't for a moment believe his account of himself. No genuine secret service man would have declared himself as such to a group of complete strangers.

He would have found some very different pretext for his comings and goings. And it is most unlikely that the name he gave the Penwarnes was his true one."

"That's very much what struck me," Arnold replied. "All the same, I have asked our Special Branch to find out if there is a secret agent, who travels to and from this country surreptitiously. What I'm wondering is whether this Mr. Battlesby, as we may continue to call him, had any association with Mr. George Hawken?"

"He might have had," said Merrion. "What's in your mind?"

"Something like this," Arnold replied. "On the day of Mr. George Hawken's death, Battlesby went ashore soon after eight. He had plenty of time to reach Cliff Cottage before nine. He saw Mr. Hawken go out, followed him, and pushed him over the cliff."

"That's possible, of course," Merrion agreed. "But what could his motive have been? Not to steal Mr. Hawken's money. According to Barry, he found that intact later in the day."

"I have an idea about motive," Arnold replied. "Battlesby and George Hawken were associated in some illegal enterprise. For some reason or other Battlesby believed that he could no longer trust his partner. He murdered him before he could give the show away."

Merrion smiled. "That is quite a good idea. But to my mind there is at least one objection to it. From what you have heard of George Hawken it seems unlikely that he should have associated with a crook. And if he did, he seems to have made nothing out of it."

"Battlesby may not be a crook," Arnold replied. "He may be merely a man who likes to keep his affairs out of the limelight."

"And George Hawken knew too much about his affairs?" Merrion asked.

"Possibly," Arnold replied. "Now another question. What were the contents of the suitcase that Battlesby always took ashore with him? Valuable documents?"

Merrion shook his head. "I doubt it. More likely something which he could sell. Here's a suggestion for you. While Battlesby was in France he bought pictures. He brought them over here for George Hawken to dispose of, possibly through his dealer friend Green. That would explain Battlesby's association with an artist."

Arnold laughed. "Your imagination again! But tell me this. Why should a business transaction like that be wrapped up in so much secrecy?" "

"There was probably some good reason," Merrion replied. "Perhaps the parties concerned did not want it to be known that the pictures had left France. I do not know enough about the picture trade to suggest why."

"I'll accept that for the moment," said Arnold. "But here's a further question. Why, if Mr. Hawken was useful to Battlesby, did he murder him?"

"It may be that Mr. Hawken's usefulness had come to an end," Merrion replied. "He may have declined to play the game any longer. Battlesby may have murdered him to ensure that he should not talk about the part he had played. Or, more likely, that Mr. Hawken should not divulge the method whereby Battlesby journeyed to and from France. But here is Newport to tell us that dinner is ready."

Merrion and Arnold went into the dining-room, where the discussion continued. "Of course, there's a snag about the Battlesby theory," said Merrion. "I am still strongly of the opinion that the same person murdered both the Hawken brothers. But I find it very difficult to understand how Battlesby can have murdered Sir Matthew. He seems to have had neither motive nor opportunity."

"I think we may agree that Battlesby cannot have murdered Sir Matthew," Arnold replied.

"Then it seems to me unlikely that he murdered George Hawken," said Merrion. "We know that he had the opportunity, but he may not have taken it. It might be profitable to try to reconstruct what actually did happen that Wednesday morning, on the assumption that Battlesby was not the murderer.

"We are told that Battlesby went ashore from Seabird soon after eight, carrying his suitcase. If he walked straight to Cliff Cottage, he would have reached there within a few minutes. George Hawken had not yet gone out, and the two men had some conversation. Battlesby emptied his suitcase, which I still think may have contained pictures. It is quite possible that the two men left the cottage together and then parted, George setting off along the cliff path with his sketching gear, and Battlesby towards the village with his empty suitcase. And now comes a question. Did Battlesby, on his way to the village, meet the murderer?"

"I hardly think that's likely," Arnold replied. "The murderer may have been approaching Cliff Cottage at the time that Battlesby left it. But he would have taken care not to meet anyone face to face. He could easily have avoided the encounter. By the roadside between the village and Cliff Cottage is a range of disused and ruinous buildings. A derelict farm, I've been told. The murderer could have hidden among these until Battlesby had gone past."

"Very well," said Merrion. "We'll drop that point for the moment. Where Battlesby went next we don't know. We are told that he did not return to Seabird until the afternoon. He probably did not hang about Port Bosun. He may have gone into Thramsbury, and spent his time there.

"But when he did get back to Seabird, he must have had something of a shock. The Penwarnes must have told him how they had recovered the body of George Hawken. They could not have resisted talking about their adventure. And the news must have given Battlesby furiously to think. His pictures were at Cliff Cottage. What was he to do about them?"

"I expect that he came to the conclusion that he could do nothing. He could safely assume that people, including the police, would be at Cliff Cottage by that time. If he made any attempt to retrieve his pictures, he would be forced to give some account of himself, and that, apparently, was the last thing he wanted to do. He would have to write off the pictures as a dead loss, at least for the present."

Arnold nodded. "I admire your reconstruction. Battlesby sailed in Seabird that evening, and transferred to the Marie Touchet in mid-Channel. He hasn't been seen by the Penwarnes since then."

"Exactly," said Merrion. "Now what, in fact, became of the pictures? George Hawken had left all his pictures to his brother. Mr. Clapdale, as his executor, would have interpreted that as meaning all the pictures which were to be found in Cliff Cottage. He would have packed up the lot, including those which were Battlesby's property, and sent them off to Moat Barn. That, no doubt, is where they are now. The question then is this. Will

Battlesby, on his next visit to Port Bosun, discover what has become of his pictures?"

"The Penwarnes may know that they had been sent to Moat Barn," Arnold replied. "But, if your theory is right, I'm beginning to wonder whether Battlesby will ever show up at Port Bosun again. Why should he? With George Hawken dead, there would be no one in the place to receive anything he brought with him."

"That's true enough," Merrion agreed. "But won't he make some attempt to recover his last consignment? I rather expect that he'll go back to Port Bosun to try to find out what has become of it. If he discovers where it has gone to, what action will he take? It is unlikely that he has heard of the death of Sir Matthew. He may well go to Moat Barn, with the intention of offering Sir Matthew some explanation."

"If he goes back to Port Bosun he'll be intercepted," Arnold replied. "The constable there has orders to keep a lookout for him. Egford will interrogate him, and he'll have to give some account of himself. But that isn't likely to happen for some two or three weeks yet. Meanwhile, what am I to do with Barry Benson?"

"You no longer believe that he murdered his uncles?" Merrion asked.

"On the whole, I don't," Arnold replied. "It is remarkable that he was more or less on the spot when both deaths occurred but, all the same, it seems more than doubtful that Barry was responsible."

"There's this to be considered," said Merrion. "While Barry is in your hands he remains inactive. If he sticks to his story, he gets you no further. On the other hand, if you set him at liberty he may take some step which will give you a clue."

"You suggest that I let him go?" Arnold asked.

"I do," Merrion replied. "Keeping him under observation, of course. I should tell him to apply to his brother, who can hardly refuse to help him out now that they are joint heirs of Sir Matthew's estate. If Barry shows signs of being difficult, you can always threaten to charge him with the theft of his Uncle George's money."

"That's not a bad idea," said Arnold. "I'll send for Barry to-morrow and have a heart to heart talk to him."

When Arnold reached Scotland Yard on Tuesday morning

he put this intention into practice. Barry was marched into the room by a constable who stood beside him during the interview.

"Well, Benson, have you still nothing to add to the statement you made last week?" Arnold asked.

Barry shook his head. "I can't add anything to the truth."

"Very well," said Arnold. "For the present, I am prepared to accept your statement as the truth. And I have decided to release you, under one condition. That is, that you report to the police every day until further notice."

This prospect did not seem to cause Barry any great joy. "But where am I to go?" he asked plaintively. "I haven't got the price of a sixpenny bus fare."

"That is unfortunate," said Arnold. "But you can't expect the taxpayer to provide you with permanent board and lodging. The best thing that you can do is to apply to your brother for temporary assistance."

"Hubert?" Barry exclaimed. "I've tried him before, and it was no good. He wouldn't lend me a penny."

"Circumstances have changed since then," said Arnold. "I may as well tell you what the present position is. Sir Matthew Hawken died intestate, and his estate therefore passes to his nearest relatives, your brother and yourself. You will in due course be in possession of considerable means."

Barry's eyes lightened up at this. "You don't mean that?" he asked incredulously.

"I do mean it," said Arnold. "Go and see your brother, and he will tell you the same thing. And if you ask him for an advance until matters are settled, he can hardly refuse you."

"I hardly care about the idea of tackling Hubert," Barry replied. "I'd rather see my sister-in-law first. She isn't so hard-hearted. But if I'm to get to Wimbledon, I shall have to walk there."

Arnold took a handful of silver from his pocket and laid it on his desk. "Come and pick that up," he said. "You can pay me back when you come into your money."

Chapter XIII

When Barry had been disposed of, Arnold took the picture which he had brought from the Green Gallery from the safe in which he had deposited it. This he placed in a brief-case and called for a police car, in which he set off for Shepherd Green.

On reaching the village, he called at the constable's house and found Jarrow at home. Arnold asked whether Sir Matthew had been buried on the previous day, and Jarrow replied that he had. Mr. Dedham had taken the service, and quite a lot of the folk living in the village had attended. Miss Paris and Albert Oakley had been there, but the chief mourner had been a gentleman who had driven down from London. Jarrow had been told that this gentleman's name was Mr. Hubert Benson. He had brought another gentleman with him, and they had both gone to Moat Barn when the funeral was over.

Arnold left the constable's house and drove on to Moat Barn, to find the drawbridge down. He supposed that since Sir Matthew's death, it had not been thought necessary to raise it. He alighted, walked up the path and knocked on the door. Albert opened it and admitted him.

"Is Miss Paris at home?" Arnold asked.

"I'm afraid not, sir," Albert replied. "Miss Paris has gone to the village to see Mr. Dedham. But she isn't likely to be very long."

"Then I'll wait for her," said Arnold. "There is no objection to my sitting in the studio?"

"None at all, sir," Albert replied. "If you will kindly take a chair?"

Mrs. Toogood, still wearing her outrageous hat, was in the studio, dusting the furniture. She replied curtly to Arnold's greeting and went on with her work.

Her manner suggested to Arnold that she was deeply upset about something. He turned to Albert. "Mr. Hubert Benson was here yesterday, I understand?" he asked.

"Yes, sir," Albert replied. "And Mr. Bridgwater came with him. Mr. Bridgwater called us together, and told us how matters stood. As Sir Matthew had destroyed his will and had not made a fresh one, all he had would go to his two nephews. Then Mr. Hubert spoke to us. He said that all expenses here must cease. He would shut up the house until he could sell it and everything that was in it. He told Miss Paris that no doubt she would make her own arrangements. I could take a month's notice, and Mrs. Toogood wouldn't be wanted after the end of the week."

Mrs. Toogood flung down her brush. "Not wanted, indeed!" she exclaimed. "It isn't for Mr. Hubert to say if I'm wanted or not. If I'd been here I'd have told him the truth. That would have put his nose out of joint good and proper."

Arnold remembered her remark about knowing something, but keeping her mouth shut. "What is the truth, Mrs. Toogood?" he asked.

But Albert interposed. "Be careful, Mrs. Toogood. Remember the promise we both made."

"Sir Matthew was alive then," she replied. "Now that he's dead, that promise doesn't bind us any longer. Unless we tell the truth now, the lady will be put upon. And you wouldn't like to see that, Mr. Oakley."

Arnold repeated his question. "What is the truth, Mrs. Toogood?"

"I'll tell you," she replied. "Sir Matthew's nephews aren't his nearest relations. His wife is. Miss Paris was married to Sir Matthew. Mr. Dedham married them, and Mr. Oakley and I were there as witnesses. That's right, isn't it, Mr. Oakley?"

She had hardly finished speaking when the door opened and Francine came in. Mrs. Toogood picked up her brush and went on with her dusting, while Albert retired to the kitchen. Francine advanced towards Arnold with a welcoming smile.

"How nice to meet you again, Mr. Arnold!" she exclaimed. "Have you come to see me? Shall we go into my room?"

Carrying his brief-case Arnold followed her into the room and shut the door. He opened the case, took from it the picture, which he handed to Francine.

"Have you ever seen that before, Miss Paris?" he asked.

"Why, of course I have," she replied. "It always hung in the studio just outside my door. Sir Matthew told me that many years ago, when the artist was unknown, he had bought it for a few guineas, but that now it was of considerable value. I can't understand how it came into your hands, Mr. Arnold?"

"Have you missed the picture since Sir Matthew's death?" Arnold asked.

Francine shook her head. "I have had too much on my mind to miss one picture out of so many."

"Then I will explain," said Arnold. "Sir Matthew's visitor on Wednesday morning was a picture dealer of the name of Green. I interviewed him, and he told me that his reason for coming here was to try to persuade Sir Matthew to sell him that picture. Sir Matthew refused to sell it, and when Green was left alone in the studio, he took down the picture and put it in his pocket. I naturally took charge of it until I could return it to its rightful owner. I now hand it over to you."

"That is most kind of you, Mr. Arnold," Francine replied.

"I have done no more than my duty," said Arnold. "I understand that Mr. Hubert Benson suggested to you yesterday that you should make your own arrangements for the future. Can you tell me what they will be?"

"Not yet," Francine replied. "I mean to consult Mr. Bridgwater before I make any plans."

"I think you are very wise," said Arnold. "Now, Miss Paris, have you nothing to tell me?"

"What do you expect me to tell you?" she replied. "I've told you everything I know already."

"Not quite everything, I think," said Arnold. "However, I cannot force you to speak if you do not wish to. Now that I have returned the picture, there is nothing to detain me here. I will say good morning."

He left the house and returned to the car. He directed the driver to the vicarage, where he alighted and rang the bell. Mrs. Welback opened the door and recognised him instantly.

"Why, Mr. Arnold, so you're back again!" she exclaimed. "You've come to see the Vicar? He's in his study, and I know he'll be glad to see you."

Arnold followed her to the study door, which she opened.

"Mr. Arnold has called to see you, sir," she announced.

Luke was sitting at his table, writing letters. He rose to his feet and stretched out his hand. "I'm delighted to see you again, Mr. Arnold," he said. "Sit down and tell me what I can do for you."

Arnold waited until Mrs. Welback had gone out and shut the door. "I have just come from Moat Barn," he replied. "There I met Mrs. Toogood, who told me the most extraordinary thing. This was that Sir Matthew and Miss Paris were married, and that you had performed the ceremony. I am bound to ask you if that was the case?"

"Mrs. Toogood's statement was perfectly correct," said Luke steadily. "She and Albert Oakley were present at the wedding, which was kept a profound secret. It was by special licence, so that no banns were called. It took place about this time last year. For some weeks past, Sir Matthew had had himself wheeled to the church, so that the village should be accustomed to see him going there. One Saturday afternoon there was a cricket match here, and most of the village were on the field watching. I performed the ceremony and Albert Oakley and Mrs. Toogood were the witnesses. Sir Matthew swore them both to secrecy."

"There can be no doubt that Sir Matthew and Miss Paris were legally married?" Arnold asked.

"None whatever," Luke replied. He rose and opened a small safe which stood in a corner of the room. From it he took a document which he handed to Arnold. "There is the marriage certificate."

Arnold studied the document, which he found to be in perfect order.

"This throws an entirely different light upon affairs." he said. "It is to be presumed that, as Sir Matthew's widow Miss Paris, as she calls herself, inherits his estate, to the exclusion of his nephews?"

"So one must suppose," Luke replied. "It will be a great disappointment to them, I fear."

"I am bound to look at the matter from another point of view," said Arnold. "There can be no doubt that Miss Paris had a better opportunity than anyone else of poisoning Sir Matthew. Her motive was not immediately apparent, but now it is perfectly clear."Luke shook his head. "I refuse to admit that Francine had any motive. She was perfectly satisfied with things as they were. I am sure that she had no ambition to inherit Sir Matthew's estate."

"Why did Sir Matthew marry her?" Arnold asked. "Did she

persuade him to?"

"Far from it," Luke replied. "Francine was at first opposed to the idea. She told me that fond as she was of Sir Matthew, she did not at all relish the prospect of being married to an octogenarian. But Sir Matthew talked her round, and in the end she consented. It was her wish that the marriage should be kept secret."

"What exactly was in Sir Matthew's mind?" Arnold asked.

Luke smiled. "That is not an easy question to answer. As you must have learnt, Sir Matthew was a curious character, and the inner workings of his mind were inscrutable. But, knowing him as I did, I think I can give you some outline. He disliked both his nephews, and was determined that they should inherit nothing of his. His collection of pictures, which he valued more than anything else in the world, he had left to his brother George. But he always had in mind the possibility that George might die before he did; as actually happened."

"What steps do you propose to take in the matter?" Arnold asked.

"The secret is out," Luke replied. "I for one am very glad, because it clarifies the situation. Without consulting Francine, I shall take it upon myself to write to Mr. Bridgwater asking him to come and see me. I shall then show him the marriage certificate. Do you agree that that is the proper course for me to take?"

"I don't see that there is any other," said Arnold. "Thank you, Mr. Dedham. I need trouble you no longer now."

Luke accompanied him to the car, and he drove back to London. As soon as he had had lunch, he rang up Merrion's rooms. Merrion answered the call and Arnold asked him when they could meet.

"You'd better come along now," Merrion replied. "I shan't be here this evening, because Mavis and I are going out."

"Then I'll come at once," said Arnold. He set out and found Merrion expecting him.

"Well, and what have you to say to me?" Merrion asked.

"I've learnt a fact so extraordinary that if I hadn't seen the proof with my own eyes, I couldn't have believed it. Miss Paris isn't Miss Paris at all. She is Sir Matthew's widow."

Merrion smiled. "Luke told me that. We wondered whether

we ought to tell you, but we decided that it would be better for you to find it out for yourself. The fact can hardly affect the course of your investigations."

"What do you mean?" Arnold exclaimed. "Of course it does. I have known all along that Miss Paris had the best opportunity of poisoning Sir Matthew. Now I know that she had the most powerful motive as well."

"I thought that you would look at it that way," said Merrion. "Have you spoken to Luke about it?"

"I have," Arnold replied. "He assures me that he is convinced of Miss Paris's innocence, a conviction with which I cannot agree. What concerns him most is the matter of the inheritance. He told me that he meant to get in touch with Mr. Bridgwater."

"And what about you?" Merrion asked. "Are you going to inform the nephews that their expectations are dashed?"

"Not I!" Arnold replied. "It's no business of mine. My job is to try to find proof of Miss Paris's guilt."

"You won't find that very easy," Merrion remarked. "If I were you, I shouldn't concentrate entirely upon her. You haven't yet solved the mystery of George Hawken's death. And it is quite obvious that Miss Paris can't have murdered him."

"For once, your imagination seems to be at fault," Arnold replied. "You stick to your theory that the same person murdered both brothers. But investigation seems to show the impossibility of that. I'm inclined to believe in two murderers acting from entirely different motives. Battlesby murdered George Hawken for some reason that we haven't yet discovered. And Miss Paris murdered Sir Matthew, in order to inherit his estate."

"You may be right about Battlesby, who seems to be something of a doubtful character," said Merrion. "But, although I have not the pleasure of Miss Paris's acquaintance, I can't somehow imagine her as a murderess. It seems to me that she would have been quite content to let things go on as they were. And she must have been genuinely fond of Sir Matthew, or she wouldn't have consented to marry him."

"That argument won't do." Arnold replied. "She may have become heartily sick of dancing attendance upon Sir Matthew. She married him in order to become his heiress. And she murdered him in order to regain her freedom."

"I'll ask you this question," said Merrion. "If Miss Paris had not married sir Matthew, would you have suspected her of his murder?"

"I suspected her from the first on the score of opportunity," Arnold replied. "But then her motive was obscure. Now it is as clear as daylight."

Merrion smiled. "It may be to you. But I look at it this way. She could have had all she wanted while Sir Matthew was alive. Why was it necessary for her to murder him?"

"She is young and most attractive." Arnold replied. "It seems to me quite possible that she was contemplating a second husband. And this time not an elderly invalid."

"There may be something in that." Merrion admitted. "But who could this man be?"

"At present I have no idea." Arnold replied. "But there is this dim possibility. She was sufficiently fond of Barry Benson to help him when his uncle had refused to do so."

"Barry Benson?" said Merrion thoughtfully. "I think that is more than a dim possibility. Wait a second while my imagination considers it."

He paused and then went on. "I still don't believe that Miss Paris was guilty but, all the same, the possibility cannot be ignored. Assuming for the moment that she was, the question arises of how she got the poison. Luke told me that she rarely or never went farther than the village, and potassium cyanide cannot be procured there. But if she has an understanding with Barry, the question can be answered. He procured it in London, and gave it to her on the day when he went to Moat Barn during his uncle's lifetime."

"If that was the case, why did she wait so long before she used it?" Arnold asked.

"For obvious reasons," Merrion replied. "If Sir Matthew had been poisoned immediately following his nephew's visit to Moat Barn, suspicion would have fallen upon Barry. And if she intended to marry him, that wouldn't have suited her book at all. So she waited for an opportunity to throw the suspicion upon someone else."

"And did that opportunity occur last Wednesday?" Arnold asked.

"She might have thought so," Merrion replied. "She saw the art dealer leaving Moat Barn, though she didn't know who or what he was. So after lunch she gave Sir Matthew the poisonous tablet, hoping that the unknown visitor would be suspected."

After they had discussed the case for some time longer, Arnold left the rooms and returned to Scotland Yard. Next morning he was told that Barry Benson had called, and asked if he might see Mr. Arnold. Arnold gave orders that he was to be brought up, and very shortly Barry appeared under escort.

"Well, Benson, what is it now?" Arnold asked.

"I've come to repay you the money you lent me yesterday, Mr. Arnold," Barry replied.

"What, already?" Arnold exclaimed. "You haven't come into your fortune yet, surely?"

"Not yet," Barry replied. "But I've managed to get hold of some money. After I left here yesterday I went to Wimbledon and saw my sister-in-law. She seemed quite pleased to see me, and told me that she and Hubert had been wondering what had become of me. I asked her if she thought that Hubert would see me if I called on him, and she said that she was sure he would. The best thing that I could do would be to go to Rutland House straight away.

"So I went, feeling not quite so optimistic as my sister-in-law seemed to be. But no sooner had his secretary told Hubert that I was there, than he told her to show me into his room. From the first, he was more affable than I had ever known him before. He told me that in future we should have to work together since we were the joint heirs of Uncle Matthew's estate. He told me that I must keep in close touch with him, and asked me where I was living.

"I said that for the moment I wasn't living anywhere, since I had no money to pay for lodgings. Very much to my surprise, Hubert told me that that was very soon got over. He counted out ten pound notes and handed them to me. Then he told me to go and find myself a room, and then come back and tell him the address.

"After I left him, I went to the Borough, to the house where I had lodged before I went to Shepherd Green. There was a room vacant, and the landlady was glad to have me back. So I took it, paying her a week in advance. Then I went back to Rutland

House, and told Hubert the address. He said that he would be responsible for the rent, but that I had better find myself a job, since it would be some time before we got anything from Uncle Matthew's estate."

"What is your address?" Arnold asked.

"Seven Mendlesham Street, S.E.1," Barry replied. "It isn't exactly Buckingham Palace, but it will suit me well enough."

"The best advice your brother gave you was to find yourself a job," said Arnold. "Have you done anything about that?"

Barry shook his head. "Not yet. I've hardly had time. But I shall go to the Labour Exchange this afternoon and see if they've got anything for me. I don't care much what it may be."

"I strongly advise you to get a job," Arnold said. "And to stick to it, this time. Now, you remember the day that you went to Moat Barn while your uncle was alive. Sir Matthew refused to see you, but Miss Paris gave you some money. Did you give her anything in return?"

"I couldn't," Barry replied. "I had nothing to give."

"Are you quite sure of that?" Arnold asked. "Didn't you give her a small package which you had brought from London?"

"Certainly I didn't," Barry replied. "I hadn't enough money to buy a package of anything."

"Miss Paris gave you some money," said Arnold. "After your return to London did you buy anything and post it to her?"

"I can't think what you're driving at, Mr. Arnold," Barry replied. "I didn't send Francine anything."

"Very well," said Arnold. "Don't forget that you are under an obligation to report daily to the police. And if you should change your address, let me know without delay. That's all now."

The constable led Barry from the room, leaving Arnold to consider what Barry had told him. He was not altogether surprised at Hubert Benson's change of heart. He would not let his brother have any money when there was no prospect of it being repaid. But now that he believed that he and Barry would share Sir Matthew's estate equally, he felt on safer ground. No doubt he regarded any money he advanced now as a loan which could be recovered later. But when he discovered how matters really stood, would his generosity persist? Arnold felt pretty sure that it wouldn't.

However, Barry's financial affairs were none of his

business. Had Barry told the truth when he declared that he had not given or sent Miss Paris anything? Arnold was inclined to think that he had. His manner had shown no sign of embarrassment. The question then remained. If Miss Paris had not obtained the poison from Barry, from whence had she obtained it?

Chapter XIV

When Arnold reached Scotland Yard on the following Friday morning, he found Wighton waiting for him.

"Well, Sergeant, what is it?" he asked.

"I have a report to make, sir," Wighton replied. "That chap Barry Benson is dead."

"Dead?" Arnold exclaimed. "What do you mean? When did he die?"

"Yesterday evening, sir," Wighton replied. "He got a knife stuck into him at a pub in the Borough. The Borough Police rang up asking for us to send some" one along, so I went. Shall I tell you what I heard about it, sir?"

"I'll hear the story at first hand," Arnold replied. "And you shall come with me. Stand by with a car. I'll be down in a minute."

After a hasty glance through the papers in his tray Arnold went down, to find Wighton standing beside a police car.

"I've told the driver where to go, sir," said Wighton.

Arnold got into the car, and they drove off. Their way took them over the river by Westminster Bridge, and then to the left into Borough High Street. The driver turned off this into a narrower street, and after following this for fifty yards or so, pulled up outside a small public-house bearing the sign of the Ninepins. The house had two doors, and outside these a constable was standing.

The constable saluted as Arnold and Wighton alighted. "We've kept the place closed this morning, sir," he said. "But the landlord is in the bar. Clacton, his name is."

"We'll go in," said Arnold. The constable rapped on one of the doors, which was very shortly opened by an agitated-looking man.

"Are you the landlord here?" Arnold asked.

"Yes, that's right," the man replied. "Will you gentlemen come in?" He stood aside to admit his visitors, then locked the door behind them. "Now tell us what happened yesterday evening," said Arnold.

"Such a thing has never happened before!" Clacton exclaimed. "I've always run this house so that there shouldn't be any trouble. It's true that I've had some tough customers now and again, but as soon as I got to know their ways, I refused to serve them, and they had to go somewhere else. I'd rather lose the price of a pint or two than risk a rough house."

"A most commendable attitude," said Arnold. "But I gather than in spite of your efforts, you did have a rough house here yesterday evening?"

"I can't understand it," Clacton replied. "We were quiet here yesterday evening, as we always are on Thursdays. My customers are apt to get spent out by that time in the week. There were only four of them in here at the time it happened. Three elderly men, who have used this house for years. I didn't know the name of the fourth, but I was told later that it was Benson. He had been in here for the last three evenings but I hadn't seen him before that.

"I was behind the counter, and the three elderly men were standing in front of it. Benson was sitting at that table yonder with a pint of mild and a couple of sandwiches. I always put up sandwiches in the evening, because plenty of my customers like a snack. There was no one in the other bar and, as I say, it was all as quiet as the grave.

"Then all at once the door by which you came in was flung open, and a man rushed in. I was never so astonished in my life. To begin with, he was wearing a mask and rubber gloves. Then he had a shabby raincoat and an even shabbier cap. As he came in he shouted, 'Down with the colour bar!' There was a bottle standing on the counter, and he picked it up and aimed a blow with it at me, but I managed to dodge aside. Then he turned to the three men standing there. He struck one of them with the bottle and knocked him down. The other two bolted out into the street."

"Wait a moment," Arnold interposed. "Before you go any further, what did the man mean? Is there any colour bar here?"

"Well, you see, it's this way," Clacton replied. "Some while ago, coloured men began to come here. I didn't refuse to serve them, but I could tell that my regular customers didn't like it. They took to keeping away, which wasn't good for my trade. I saw that something must be done about it, so that the coloured men shouldn't annoy the regular customers.

"I consulted the brewers about it, and they agreed to my suggestion. This partition was put up, dividing the bar into two. The partition ends at the counter, which runs through both bars, so that I can serve customers in either. And another door was put up, so each bar had a separate entrance. The regulars use this bar, and the coloured men the other."

"And how does the arrangement work?" Arnold asked.

"Very well," Clacton replied. "I thought that perhaps the coloured men wouldn't like being shut off, as it were. But they don't mind. In fact, I think they rather like being by themselves. I've had no complaints until yesterday evening, when that chap came in and kicked up a disturbance."

"He must have supposed that he had a grievance," said Arnold. "Go on and tell me what happened next."

"It was all over so quickly that it's hard to tell what exactly did happen," Clacton replied. "As I've told you, the chap knocked down one of the customers standing at the counter. Then Benson jumped up and went for him. I suppose he meant to snatch the bottle from his hand. But as Benson was crossing the bar towards him, he put his hand under his raincoat and drew out a knife. I think that Benson tried to snatch his arm, but he wasn't quick enough. The man made a dart at him, and drove the knife into his chest up to the hilt. Benson fell to the floor, and the chap dashed out into the street, leaving the knife where it was."

"And what did you do?" Arnold asked.

"The first thing that I did was to come round into the bar to see if I could do anything for Benson," Clacton replied. "When I saw that I couldn't, I came back, rang up the police, and told them what had happened. They were here in no time, and took charge. The man who had been knocked down had a nasty crack on the head, and was feeling very sorry for himself. The police sent for an ambulance and he was taken away to hospital. Then the police surgeon came along and examined Benson. He said that he was dead, and must have been killed instantly. Then the inspector in charge of the party rang up Scotland Yard."

"That's where you come in, Sergeant," said Arnold. "What is your report?"

"I started off straight away, sir," Wighton replied. "It didn't take me long to get here. I found an inspector of the Borough Police in charge, and he told me that the body had just been taken to the mortuary. I took a statement from Mr. Clacton, and the inspector said that he would get statements from the three customers who were in the bar when the masked man burst in."

Arnold turned to Clacton. "Do you suppose that the man was coloured?" he asked.

"I think it's very likely that he was," Clacton replied. "He wouldn't have hollered out about the colour bar if he'd been white. But I couldn't see his skin or whether his hair was curly. The mask was over his face, the cap was over his hair, and he was wearing gloves. What I did notice about him was his voice when he sang out. It was just like a woman's."

"Can it have been a woman dressed as a man?" Arnold asked.

"That I couldn't say," Clacton replied. "If it was a woman, she must be mighty strong in the arm. The blow from the bottle knocked my customer flat. And it must take some strength to drive a knife into a man's body up to the hilt."

"That's quite right," Arnold agreed. "Were there many people in the street while this was going on?"

"I didn't go out to look," Clacton replied dryly. "But it's not likely that there were many folk about. There were plenty in the High Street, I don't doubt. But, except on Saturdays, there aren't many about in the evening in our street."

"The man made himself conspicuous by wearing a mask," said Arnold. "It's more than likely that he was seen, coming in or going out."

"I beg your pardon, sir," Wighton replied. "When I was here yesterday evening the inspector showed me a mask. One of his men had found it lying on the pavement five yards from here in the direction of the High Street."

"The inspector showed it to me," said Clacton. "It was just like the one the man was wearing."

Arnold nodded. "Then it's pretty clear what happened. The man pulled off his mask and dropped it as soon as he got outside. And I rather expect that he slipped it on just before he burst in. So that, after all, no one in the street may have seen him wearing it. Well, Sergeant, it's time we were moving on."

He and Wighton left the Ninepins and got into the car, Arnold telling the driver to drive to the mortuary. They reached the place, and the attendant admitted them. He took them to a slab on which lay a body covered by a sheet. This he withdrew, revealing the body lying on its back. Protruding from the left side of the chest was the handle of what appeared to be a domestic kitchen knife.

"The doctor said that it was to be left like that until the pathologist had seen it," the attendant explained.

Arnold looked long and searchingly at the dead man's face.

"Yes, it's Barry all right," he said. "Well, at least he's been spared the disappointment that was coming to him, poor chap. We shall have to break the news to his brother, I suppose. But first of all I'd like to hear what the local police have to say."

They left the mortuary, and drove to Southwark Police Station. Arnold asked the sergeant on duty who was in charge of the Ninepins case, and was told that it was Inspector Marden. Arnold and Wighton were taken to his room. Marden recognised Wighton, who introduced him to Arnold.

"I'm very pleased to meet you, Mr. Arnold," said Marden. "You've come to talk to me about that affair at the Ninepins?"

"That is so," Arnold replied. "To begin with, what sort of reputation has the Ninepins?"

"A very good one," said Marden. "We have never had any trouble with the house, and Clacton, the landlord, is a steady, law abiding chap, who won't stand for any rowdiness. He has fixed up a separate bar for his coloured customers, mainly with the idea of keeping them out of harm's way. Some of the tough young cockneys seem to resent their presence in the Borough."

"Are there many of them round here?" Arnold asked.

"Quite a few," Marden replied. "They get rough jobs easily enough. Porters, street cleaners, and that sort of thing."

"Have you any idea who the masked man may have been?" Arnold asked.

"His reference to the colour bar suggests that he was a coloured man with a grievance," Marden replied. "Some of them do carry knives, carefully hidden, of course. If any of them are caught carrying a knife, the reply is always that they only carry them for self-defence, in case they should be set upon by a gang of hooligans. I imagine that the masked man used his knife on

Barry Benson because he thought he was going to be beaten up."

"I had been in touch with Barry for some days past," said Arnold. "How was it that you identified him?"

"I recognised him at once," Marden replied. "He had reported here on the previous three days, on your instructions, he told me. Had you anything against him?"

"I had reason to believe that he might have been concerned in two murders," said Arnold. "And by his own admission, he had been guilty of theft. That is why I didn't want to lose sight of him."

"Do you know whether he had any relations?" Marden asked.

"His brother is a prosperous businessman," Arnold replied. "I've met him, and I'll make it my business to break the news to him. Do you want any help in hunting down the masked man?"

"I hardly think it's necessary," said Marden. "He must live in this neighbourhood, or he wouldn't have burst into the Ninepins like that. I've already started a comb out through the Borough. The trouble is going to be that if any of his fellow-countrymen know anything, they'll be careful to keep their knowledge to themselves."

"That's only to be expected," Arnold agreed. "May I have a look at that mask that your man picked up?"

Marden took the mask from a drawer of his desk and handed it to Arnold. It was a most primitive affair. Merely a square of black silk, unhemmed, with two slits cut in it for the eyes. Clumsily sewn on to the top corners was a length of elastic, which could be slipped over the back of the head to keep the mask in position.

"No woman made that mask," Arnold remarked as he handed it back.

"It doesn't look like it," Marden replied. "Did you think that there was a woman mixed up in the affair?"

"Only for this reason," said Arnold. "Clacton told me that the voice was just like a woman. It occurred to me that the wearer of the mask might have been a woman dressed as a man."

"Well, I suppose it's possible," Marden replied. "Some of the coloured women in this neighbourhood are regular Amazons.

But they aren't as a rule as colour conscious as the men. My own idea is that the wearer of the mask was a half-crazy coloured man. He had probably had a drink or two at some other pub, and that inflamed his blood. I'll let you know at once if we get any sort of clue."

Arnold and Wighton left the police station and returned to the car. "We'll have a word with Barry's landlady," said Arnold. "Tell the driver to find his way to Mendlesham Street."

Mendlesham Street turned out to be the next street to the one in which the Ninepins was situated. Number seven was a squalid looking house, with a card in one of the windows bearing the word 'Apartments." Arnold knocked on the door, which was opened by a slatternly woman. "I've got a back room empty, if that's what you're wanting," she said.

Arnold shook his head. "I don't want a room, thanks. I am a police officer making inquiries. Did Barry Benson lodge here?"

"That he did, poor man," the woman replied. "I couldn't make out why he didn't come home last night. It was only this morning that I heard he'd been knifed in a set-to at the Ninepins. That's how it is that I've got an empty room. If you want to talk about Barry Benson you'd best come in."

Arnold and Wighton followed her into an untidy kitchen, which smelt strongly of boiling cabbage. "Was Barry Benson in the habit of going to the Ninepins?" Arnold asked.

"Every evening since he was here," the woman replied. "The first time he stayed here, which was last week, he asked me where he could get a snack and a drop of beer to wash it down with. You see, I don't cook meals for my lodgers, except a bit of breakfast. I told him he couldn't do better than the Ninepins, in the next street. I knew of it, because my husband often goes there. He wasn't there yesterday evening, because he'd gone to see a pal of his in Lambeth."

"When did you last see Benson?" Arnold asked.

"Yesterday afternoon," she replied. "All my other lodgers were out at work, and he seemed lonely, so I asked him in here for a cup of tea. There's few I'd do that for, but he was always so quiet and good tempered. And while we were having our tea he asked me if I knew of any job going that would suit him.

"I told him that I did know of a job, but whether it would suit him or not I couldn't tell. You see, it was this way. My husband's cousin, who lives in this street, has worked for some time as a porter in a block of flats in Putney. But he is giving up the job, because it's so far for him to come and go. He's got another job as a drayman at the brewery nearby. I told Barry Benson that as far as I knew, the porter's job was open, and that he'd better go to the block and ask. He said he'd go there this morning. But now someone else will get the job. I'm not owed any money, for Barry Benson paid me a week in advance."

"Have you any coloured lodgers?" Arnold asked.

"Coloured?" she exclaimed. "Not likely. My other lodgers would very soon give notice if I had coloured men in the house. They may be human beings the same as us, but black and white don't mix easily."

"Did Benson have any visitors while he was with you?" Arnold asked.

The woman shook her head. "Nobody came to see him, if that's what you mean. But it wasn't that he had no relations. He told me that he had a brother who was helping him. And he said that he didn't expect to be here very long. Only until he got a lot of money that was coming to him from an uncle who had died."

Arnold thanked her, and he and Wighton left the house.

"Rutland House now," said Arnold as they entered the car. "We shall see how Hubert Benson takes the news of his brother's death. Quite calmly, I expect, because he will believe that he is now his uncle's sole heir."

They reached Rutland House, and were shown into Hubert's presence. He received them without enthusiasm.

"Well, and what is it now, Mr. Arnold?" he asked brusquely. "You always contrive to come here when I am at my busiest."

"We shall not take up much of your time, Mr. Benson," Arnold replied. "We are, I regret to say, the bearers of bad news. Your brother Barry died yesterday evening."

"Barry dead?" Hubert exclaimed incredulously. "He was well enough when I saw him a day or two ago. What did he die of?"

"He was stabbed to death in a public-house," Arnold replied. "You will, I hope, allow me to express my sympathy. I shall have to ask you to view the body, which is in the Borough mortuary, so that you will be able to give evidence of identification at the inquest."

"Another interruption to my work," Hubert growled. "But I

suppose it can't be helped. I will make time to pay a visit to the mortuary. Fancy Barry having allowed himself to get mixed up in a brawl in a low public-house! And now, Mr. Arnold, I must ask you to excuse me. Mr. Bridgwater rang me up and asked for an appointment in half an hour's time. I expect he wants to consult me upon some matter concerning my uncle's estate. I shall have to inform him of Barry's death."

"You will be in London for the next few days?" Arnold asked. "I will inform you as soon as possible of the date and time of the inquest."

"I shall be here for the next few days," Hubert replied. "But in the course of next week or so, I shall be going to the Continent on one of my periodical visits. May I remind you that I am a very busy man, Mr. Arnold?"

Arnold took the hint, and he and Wighton left Rutland House, and returned to Scotland Yard. As soon as he reached his room, Arnold put a call through to Merrion's rooms. It was a forlorn hope, because it was probable that Merrion had gone back to High Eldersham Hall. But, much to his satisfaction, Merrion himself answered. "This is Arnold speaking. I didn't really expect to find you still in London."

"Mavis went home yesterday," Merrion replied. "But some business cropped up, and I'm staying here over the week-end. What do you want with me? Is there any fresh development in the Hawken case?"

"There is indeed," said Arnold. "Barry Benson has been killed, and I should like to tell you about it."

"I shall be out all the afternoon," Merrion replied. "You had better come and have dinner with me this evening, if that will suit you."

Arnold replied that it would suit him very well. At half-past seven he presented himself at Merrion's rooms, where he was regaled with a glass of sherry. "Well, tell me about the unfortunate Barry," said Merrion.

Arnold told him what he had learnt in the course of the morning. "It was just sheer bad luck," he went on. "If Barry hadn't tried to take the bottle away from the intruder, he wouldn't have been knifed. I'm pretty sure that the man wouldn't have drawn his knife if he hadn't thought that Barry was going to assault him."

"Perhaps not," said Merrion. "Had Barry been up to any mischief since he had been lodging in the Borough? He hadn't been beating up the coloured population, for instance?"

"Not that I know of," Arnold replied. "And I think it's most unlikely. His landlady spoke of him as being quiet and well behaved. And he certainly didn't cause trouble at the Ninepins. If he had, Clacton would have turned him out. He had been there on the two previous evenings. His landlady had recommended the Ninepins to him as a place where he could get a snack and a pint of beer with it."

"You think that the masked man would have knifed anyone who went for him?" Merrion asked.

"I'm sure of it," Arnold replied. "This is how I see it. The intruder was a coloured man who had a bee in his bonnet about the colour bar. To his mind Clacton was a supporter of the bar, since he had had a partition put up to separate his white from his coloured customers. You must remember that the intruder aimed his first blow at Clacton. Since that blow missed, he turned on the three white men standing by the counter. He knocked one of them down, and the other two bolted from the house.

"If Barry had remained seated where he was, the intruder might have gone for him, with the bottle, not with the knife, which he probably regarded as a weapon of defence. But Barry went for him first, and got knifed for his pains."

"You may be right," said Merrion. "But this point occurs to me. One can understand the man wearing a mask. But why should he have been wearing gloves? Doesn't that suggest that he intended to use his knife without leaving his fingerprints on the hilt?"

"Not necessarily," Arnold replied. "He meant to use something as a weapon, and he guessed that in a pub he would find ready to his hand a bottle, or a heavy tankard, which would have suited his purpose equally well. He didn't mean to leave his fingerprints on whatever weapon he did find."

"That may be so," Merrion agreed. "In any case he seems to be a pretty desperate character. You're doing your best to trace him, I take it?"

"I'm leaving that to the Borough people," Arnold replied. "They know the folk in their division better than we at the Yard do. But the trouble is going to be that these birds of a coloured feather flock together, and none of them would give another away. However, Marden is doing his best, and with luck he may get results."

"Let's hope that he does," said Merrion. "I gather from what you tell me that Hubert Benson shed no tears on hearing the news of his brother's death?"

"He barely batted an eyelid," Arnold replied. "His remark to me implied that he considered it to have been Barry's fault for frequenting low pubs. Not that the Ninepins is a low pub. On the contrary, it is a highly respectable one."

"It is easy to understand Hubert's complacency," Merrion remarked. "When you broke the news to him, he believed that Barry's death would leave him his uncle's sole heir."

Arnold chuckled. "He'll have learnt the truth by now. I don't like the fellow, and I can't sympathise with his disappointment. But I should have liked to have been present at his interview with Mr. Bridgwater. Just to see how he took it."

Chapter XV

The inquest on Barry Benson took place on the following Monday morning, the coroner sitting with a jury. The first witness called was Hubert. He had viewed the body, and recognised it as that of his younger brother, Barry Benson, aged thirty-seven, and of no fixed address. He understood that at the time of his death he had been lodging at seven Mendlesham Street. He had last seen his brother on the previous Tuesday, when he had been in his normal health and spirits. Asked by the coroner who his brother's employers were, Hubert replied that as far as he was aware, his brother had been out of employment.

Clacton followed, and gave a vivid account of the affray at the Ninepins. He had no idea of the identity of the masked man, who had escaped before he could be intercepted.

The next witness was the injured customer, his head swathed in bandages. His account of the affair was couched in picturesque language.

"The chap came barging in, hollering out something about a colour bar. There was a bottle on the counter, and he picked it up and swiped at Mr. Clacton with it. Mr. Clacton managed to dodge, and then he turned on me. Bashed me on the head with the bottle, he did, though I'd never done him any harm. I don't remember any more after that, till I woke up to find myself in hospital."

"You are a regular customer of the Ninepins, I understand," said the coroner. "Have you ever before known any disturbance there?"

"I've never known no disturbance," the witness replied. "Mr. Clacton isn't the sort to put up with anything like that. If any of his customers turned nasty, which wasn't often, he'd chuck them out on the spot."

The two uninjured customers followed in succession. They gave their evidence rather sheepishly, obviously ashamed of the fact that they had taken to flight. They described the entrance of the masked man, and his shout about the colour bar. Both admitted that as soon as he had struck down their companion, they had bolted. One of them remarked, in palliation of his cowardice, "He'd got hold of that blessed bottle, and we'd got only our bare fists."

The medical evidence was then taken. First the police surgeon. He had had a call from the police to go to the Ninepins. There he had found the deceased lying on the floor, with the hilt of a knife protruding from his chest. On examination, he had found that he was dead. He had not removed the knife, and had arranged for the body to be taken to the mortuary. A second man, who had appeared as a witness, was lying on the floor. He was unconscious, and had a contusion above the forehead. An ambulance had been summoned to take him to hospital.

The pathologist came next. He had examined the body of the deceased in the mortuary on Friday afternoon. The knife which had penetrated the body was in position, and from the direction which it had taken, he could see that it had reached the heart. He had performed a post-mortem, which confirmed that this had been the case. The heart had been penetrated to the depth of two inches. He had no doubt that this had been the cause of death.

Marden was the last witness called. He described his arrival at the Ninepins and what he had found there. He produced the knife, which he exhibited to the coroner and jury. It was an ordinary kitchen knife, but with an exceptionally sharp point. Marden gave it as his opinion that it had been sharpened quite recently. It had been examined for fingerprints but none had been found on it. This could be explained by the fact that the man who had struck with it had been wearing gloves. Efforts to trace this man were being continued, but so far without result.

The coroner addressed the jury. They would have no difficulty in deciding on the cause of death. They might come to the conclusion that the assailant had stabbed the deceased in self-defence. But even if that had been the case, he remained responsible for the death of the deceased. They were at liberty to retire if they wished to do so.

The members of the jury whispered among themselves. In less than a couple of minutes the foreman rose to his feet. The jury did not find it necessary to retire. Their unanimous verdict was that the deceased had been murdered by some person unknown.

The coroner expressed his agreement with that verdict, and his sympathy with the relatives of the deceased. It was sincerely to be hoped that the police would be successful in tracking down the murderer. He made out a burial certificate, which he handed to Hubert, who received it with obvious reluctance.

Merrion had attended the inquest, and he and Arnold left the court together.

"You'd better come round to my place and have a spot of lunch," said Merrion. "It won't be a waste of your time, because you'll have to lunch somewhere."

Arnold accepted the invitation, and they took a taxi to Merrion's rooms. "Well, what did you think of it?" Arnold asked, as Merrion produced a couple of bottles of beer.

"I found the atmosphere of the court close and stuffy," Merrion replied. "It has given me a thirst which only beer will quench."

"I feel the same," Arnold agreed. "But what I meant was, what did you think of the evidence and the verdict?"

"I've no quarrel with either," Merrion replied. "The evidence was perfectly straightforward, and the witnesses didn't contradict one another. As for the verdict, it was the only one possible."

"It was bad luck on Barry," said Arnold. "If he had bolted with the other two, he'd have been alive now. As it is, he's dead, and Hubert is left with the job of burying him. I don't suppose that he relishes the idea of paying for his brother's funeral. Especially as he knows now that he'll get nothing from his uncle's estate. But, so far as I am concerned, Barry's death is only an interlude. It doesn't help me with the Hawken case."

"If it could be proved that Barry murdered his uncles, that case would be at an end," Merrion replied.

"I don't believe he did," said Arnold. "Are you still of the opinion that both Hawkens were murdered by the same person?"

"I am," Merrion replied. "It would be astonishing if the two brothers had been murdered by different people."

"Then who can that person have been?" Arnold asked. "Leaving Barry out of it, this is the situation. Battlesby had the opportunity, and possibly the motive, for murdering George

Hawken. But he cannot have poisoned Sir Matthew. Miss Paris, or Lady Hawken, as I suppose we ought to call her, had every opportunity and motive for poisoning her husband. But by no possibility can she have pushed George Hawken over the cliff."

"Then the murderer must be some person who has not yet come under suspicion," Merrion replied. "Have you given any thought to Hubert Benson? He had, or believed he had, a motive for murdering his uncles. George, because Sir Matthew had left him the most valuable part of his estate, and Sir Matthew, because he believed that he would die an intestate bachelor."

"I have given considerable thought to Hubert whom, I repeat, I dislike," said Arnold. "But he doesn't fit in. There is no doubt whatever that he was on the Continent when George Hawken died, and that he was in London when Sir Matthew was poisoned."

"Leave him out, then," Merrion replied. "That disposes of both the Benson brothers. We have then to find some other person. But isn't it possible that you're on the wrong track, so far at least as George Hawken is concerned?"

"What do you mean?" Arnold replied.

"Just this," Merrion said. "You have no definite proof that George Hawken was murdered."

"If he wasn't, how did he come by that mark round his neck?" said Arnold. "Apart from that, how did he come by his death? Everyone who knew him says that he was the last person to commit suicide. And it is very hard to believe that he fell from the cliff accidentally."

"It may be hard to believe," Merrion replied. "But it is still possible. And there is this to be considered. If George Hawken's death was accidental, you have no further need to look for some person who had the opportunity of murdering both him and Sir Matthew."

"If that were the case, I should plump for Lady Hawken," said Arnold. "I shall go down to Moat Barn to-morrow and have it out with her."

"I should very much like to see the interior of that queer place," Merrion replied. "And, incidentally, the pictures. How would it be if I were to drive you down there?"

"I should like nothing better," said Arnold. "And you could be present at my interview with Lady Hawken. I shall be interested to hear what impression she makes upon you."

Merrion smiled. "Perhaps I shall fall under the fascination of her charm. And while we are at Moat Barn, it might be worth your while to have another interview with Albert Oakley."

"Do you suppose that he comes into the picture?" Arnold asked.

"I think that he may be right in the foreground," Merrion replied. "It has been generally assumed that the poison which proved fatal to Sir Matthew was contained in the tablet which his wife gave him after lunch. But there is no proof of that."

"In what else could the poison have been contained?" Arnold asked.

"In Sir Matthew's helping of gooseberry-pie," Merrion replied. "It is to be noted that neither of the lunch dishes were brought to the table. Albert helped them in the kitchen, and brought the helpings into the studio. Albert could have introduced some potassium cyanide into the helping he brought to Sir Matthew."

"We've considered that possibility before," said Arnold. "The question remains of why Albert should have done such a thing. He had no motive whatever for poisoning Sir Matthew."

"Hadn't he?" Merrion replied. "While it was believed that his nephews would inherit Sir Matthew's estate, Albert seemed to have no motive. In fact it appeared that Sir Matthew's death would be of the gravest disadvantage to him. But the fact that he was in the secret of the marriage throws a different light upon the affair. He knew that Lady Hawken would become her husband's heiress. And he felt pretty certain that she would either present him with the legacy mentioned in the first will, or support him for the rest of his life."

"I hadn't looked at it that way," said Arnold. "Do you think that there can have been any collusion between Lady Hawken and Albert?"

"I think that's most unlikely/' Merrion replied. "If either of them poisoned Sir Matthew, they probably acted on his or her own. I've only presented you with a possibility. You may be able to form an opinion when we've been to Moat Barn."

On Tuesday morning Merrion drove Arnold to Shepherd Green.

"I see no reason for calling on Luke Dedham now," said

Merrion as they reached the village. "Perhaps we may later on. It will be best to go on to Moat Barn and see if Lady Hawken is at home."

They went on, alighted at the drawbridge, which now seemed to be permanently down, and walked up the path to the house. Arnold knocked on the door which was opened by Albert.

"Is Lady Hawken at home?" Arnold asked.

Albert seemed completely taken aback. It was probable that he had never thought of Francine as Lady Hawken. However, he recovered himself.

"She is sitting on the terrace, sir," he replied. "Shall I tell her that you have called?"

"If you will, please," said Arnold. Albert went off, and Arnold and Merrion entered the studio, round which Merrion strolled, looking at the pictures. In two or three minutes Francine appeared, looking at her best in a plain black dress.

"So you have come to see me again, Mr. Arnold?" she asked.

"I have," Arnold replied, "and this time I have brought a friend with me. Mr. Merrion, who is helping me in my investigations. May we have a talk with you?"

"Come into my room," said Francine. Arnold and Merrion followed her, and were asked to sit down. "What do you want to talk about?" she asked.

"This, first of all," said Arnold. "Why, when I was last here, did you not tell me that you had been married to Sir Matthew?"

Francine's reply was prompt and frank. "Because, if I had, you would have suspected me of having poisoned Matthew. And I believe that it is because you do suspect me, that you have come here to-day."

"I am bound to suspect anyone who had motive and opportunity," said Arnold. "You, Lady Hawken, had both. Did Barry Benson ever give or send you any poison?"

"Never!" she exclaimed. "And, if he had, I shouldn't have used it to kill Matthew. Why should I? I was very fond of Matthew, whom I regarded rather as a father than a husband, and I was perfectly happy living here with him."

"Was it at your instigation that Sir Matthew married you?" Arnold asked:

"Far from it," she replied. "Matthew asked me again and again to marry him, but I refused. The disparity between our ages seemed too ridiculous. Mr. Dedham, in whom Matthew confided, can tell you that that is true. But at last I consented, because I could see that Matthew's heart was set upon it."

"You improved your future prospects very considerably by marrying Sir Matthew," Arnold remarked.

"That consideration never entered my head," Francine replied. "And my prospects were not so greatly improved. By Matthew's first will, which he made before we were married, he had left me enough to provide me with a comfortable income. By Matthew's death I lost not only a husband but a very dear friend."

"If you did not poison Sir Matthew, who did?" Arnold asked.

Francine shook her head. "Naturally, I have asked myself that question night and day. But I cannot imagine who could have done it."

"Have you ever suspected Albert Oakley?" Arnold asked.

"I cannot suspect him," Francine replied. "I know that he could have done it, but why should he? What could he have hoped to gain by Matthew's death? He knew that the will which provided him with a legacy had been destroyed. When Matthew died, he lost his employer, and he is too old to find another place. Apart from all that, Albert was devoted to Matthew."

"Then we'll change the subject," said Arnold. "Are you aware that Barry Benson was killed last week?"

"Barry killed?" Francine exclaimed. "No, I was not aware of it, and I'm terribly sorry. Barry may have been a vagabond, as Matthew called him, but I always had a warm spot in my heart for him. How did it happen?"

"One might say by accident," said Arnold. "He was trying to disarm a total stranger who was making a disturbance in a public-house, and the man turned upon him and stabbed him."

"How dreadful!" Francine exclaimed. "I meant to do something for Barry when Matthew's money was in my hands. I thought that I might buy him a partnership in a small business, or something like that. Then he would have something definite to do, without having to drift from one job to another. I felt quite sure that if he had something to interest him, he would stick to it."

"You preferred Barry to Hubert?" Arnold asked.

"Infinitely," Francine replied. "I have never liked Hubert,

and his behaviour here after Matthew's funeral was disgusting. He threw his weight about as though he was already the owner of the place. I'm glad to know that by now he has been disillusioned."

"Have you decided on your plans for the future, Lady Hawken?" Arnold asked.

"I have made up my mind to stay here," Francine replied. "I think that it was what Matthew would have liked me to do. And I shall of course keep on both Albert and Mrs. Toogood. Mr. Bridgwater was here yesterday, and I told him that that was what I meant to do."

"Did Mr. Bridgwater mention Hubert Benson?" Arnold asked.

"He told me that he had seen Hubert last Friday," Francine replied. "He said that he had explained to Hubert how matters stood, and that I was Matthew's heiress. I'm afraid that Hubert must have been terribly disappointed. Though he deserved it, after the way he had behaved."

"Did Mr. Bridgwater say nothing of Barry Benson?" Arnold asked.

Francine shook her head. "Not a word. He can't have known that Barry had been killed, or he would certainly have told me."

"Thank you, Lady Hawken," said Arnold. "You have no objection to our talking to Albert Oakley?"

"None whatever," Francine replied. "You are sure to find him in the kitchen."

Arnold and Merrion left the room and crossed the studio to the kitchen, where they found Albert polishing silver.

"Listen to me, Oakley," said Arnold. "You know perfectly well that the only people in the house when Sir Matthew was poisoned were you and Lady Hawken. What have you to say to that?"

"It's perfectly true, sir," Albert replied. "But Lady Hawken didn't poison the master, that I'll swear. She was far too fond of him to do a thing like that. She was struck all of a heap when she found that he was dead."

"And what about yourself?" Arnold asked. "You could so easily have slipped some poison into Sir Matthew's helping of gooseberry-pie."

"I?" Albert exclaimed. "Was it likely that I would poison the master I'd been with so long, and who had always been so kind to me? Besides, Sir Matthew didn't eat the helping of pie I gave him."

"What do you mean?" Arnold asked. "That he left the helping on his plate?"

"No, I don't mean that," Albert replied. "This was the way of it. I helped two portions, a fairly big one for Sir Matthew, because I knew that he liked gooseberry-pie, and a smaller one for Lady Hawken. I took these into the studio and put them on the table. Then Sir Matthew said that I'd given him too much, and Lady Hawken not enough. He passed his plate to Lady Hawken and took hers."

"You're quite sure of that?" Arnold asked.

"Quite sure," Albert replied. "So that if I'd put poison into Sir Matthew's helping, it would have been Lady Hawken who died. I expect that she remembers Sir Matthew changing over his plate of gooseberry pie for her plate."

As Arnold and Merrion left the kitchen, they saw Francine crossing the studio. Arnold went up to her. "One more word, Lady Hawken," he said. "You remember lunching with Sir Matthew on the day of his death?"

"I remember it very well," Francine replied. "Little did I think that it would be our last meal together."

"Did Sir Matthew change anything in the course of that meal?" Arnold asked.

Francine looked slightly puzzled. "What sort of thing? He didn't alter any of our arrangements. But I remember now that he did change something. When Albert brought in the gooseberry-pie, Matthew said that he had given him too much and me too little. So he changed our plates round. Is that what you mean?"

"It is exactly what I mean," said Arnold. "Thank you, Lady Hawken. We won't intrude on you any longer now."

He and Merrion left the house and returned to the car. "I should like to call on Mr. Dedham now," said Arnold. "You can guess why."

"I can," Merrion replied. "Come along then, and we'll drive to the vicarage."

When they reached the vicarage, Mrs. Welback told them that the vicar was at home, and took them to his study.

"Well!" Luke exclaimed as they were shown in. "This is indeed an unexpected pleasure. Come in and sit down both of you. Are you on your way to Moat Barn?"

"We have just come from there," Arnold replied. "You won't mind if I ask you a question, Mr. Dedham? Is it a fact that Lady Hawken hesitated for some time before she agreed to marry Sir Matthew?"

"It is a fact," said Luke. "I can vouch for that, for both of them told me their point of view. Sir Matthew wanted to marry Francine anyway. But there was an additional reason: he wanted to make sure that, whatever might happen, his nephews should never inherit anything of his.

"There is no doubt that Francine was devoted to Sir Matthew, and she told me that she would undertake to look after him for the rest of his life without being married to him. But she feared they would both make themselves laughing stocks if she married a man old enough to be her grandfather. She didn't care in the least what people said about her. As for the nephews, Sir Matthew had already made a will cutting them out.

"So it went on for some months. But Sir Matthew was one of those people who always seem to get their own way in the long run, and at last Francine gave in. She told me that Sir Matthew wanted the marriage so badly that she hadn't the heart to hold out any longer. Both of them wanted the marriage to be kept secret, and so it was, until Mrs. Toogood blurted out the secret to you, Mr. Arnold."

"You do not believe that Lady Hawken poisoned her husband, Mr. Dedham?" Arnold asked.

"I steadfastly refuse to believe anything of the kind," Luke replied. "Apart from the fact that the uprightness of her character makes it impossible that she should have done such a thing, she is and was genuinely distressed by Sir Matthew's death."

After some further conversation Arnold and Merrion left the vicarage and started on their drive back to London.

"What did you make of what we heard at Moat Barn?" Arnold asked.

"The first thing that struck me was that Lady Hawken had not been told of Barry's death," Merrion replied. "Since Mr.

Bridgwater was there yesterday, that seems most extraordinary. You broke the news to Hubert on Friday morning. Shortly afterwards he had his interview with Mr. Bridgwater. If he had told the lawyer of Barry's death, Mr. Bridgwater would have passed the news on to Lady Hawken. Why didn't Hubert tell him?"

Arnold laughed. "He was too flabbergasted when he had heard what Mr. Bridgwater had to say to him that such trifles as the death of his brother passed from his mind. What else struck you?"

"The obvious innocence of both Lady Hawken and Albert Oakley," Merrion replied. "They knew that they were the principal suspects. You left neither of them in any doubt about that. If either of them had been guilty, he or she would have tried to incriminate the other. Instead of which, both of them declared that the other would never have committed the crime.

"Then we come to that curious accident of the changing of the plates. If Albert had added poison to the helping he set before Sir Matthew, it would, as he so sagely pointed out, have been fatal to Lady Hawken. On the other hand, is it likely that he added poison to the helping he intended for Lady Hawken? I think not. He had nothing to gain by her death. In fact, it would probably have led to the nephews inheriting Sir Matthew's estate. And that no one desired, except the nephews themselves, least of all Albert. In my opinion, Albert is completely cleared."

"And you are equally convinced of Lady Hawken's innocence?" Arnold asked.

"Under the circumstances I am," Merrion replied. "I can see no earthly reason why she should have desired the death of her husband."

"Isn't it possible that she poisoned him because she wanted to marry Barry?" Arnold asked.

Merrion shook his head. "I feel sure that we can bury that theory in the depths of oblivion. She was certainly shocked when you told her of Barry's death. But her manner showed that the shock was due to friendship, not to love. Her reaction was far from being that of a woman who has lost her lover. She was able to talk about Barry quite dispassionately. If she had intended to marry him, she could hardly have concealed her emotions."

"Very well, then," said Arnold. "But tell me this. If the two people who had the opportunity are cleared, who was the poisoner?"

"I have my idea about that," Merrion replied. "It seems to me that the clue is more likely to come from Port Bosun than Moat Barn. Will you let me know immediately if Battlesby comes to the surface again?"

"Certainly, if you want me to," said Arnold. "But I would point out that though Battlesby may have murdered George Hawken, he can't possibly have poisoned Sir Matthew."

"Never mind," Merrion replied. "Now look here. I am going home to-morrow, and I shall be at High Eldersham Hall until further notice. If you hear that Battlesby has landed, ring me up and tell me. I will then drive to London at once, pick you up, and take you to Port Bosun. What do you think of that plan?"

"It will suit me down to the ground," said Arnold. "Very well, then," said Merrion. "That's settled."

Chapter XVI

Docking, nothing if not conscientious, carried out his instructions faithfully. Whenever Seabird put to sea, he asked one of the Penwarnes quite casually, when they expected to return to port.

His routine was quite simple. He knew that Seabird could enter or leave the harbour during a limited period, from two hours before high water till two hours after. He had only to look up the tide table to ascertain when this period would be. On sailing days Docking would stroll down to the quay and engage one of the Penwarnes in conversation. He was on good terms with all the brothers, and they had no reason to hide their comings and goings from him. He would learn on what date Seabird, barring accidents, would return, and he would know at what time of day to keep a lookout for her.

For several weeks Docking persevered in his routine, without anything abnormal happening. The news of Barry's death had spread to Port Bosun. On the Friday following the event Arnold had rung up Superintendent Egford, told him what had happened. Egford in turn had rung up Docking, and told him to inform Mr. Clapdale. Paul had received the news in some consternation. What was he, as George Hawken's sole surviving executor, to do about Cliff Cottage? He supposed that it would now go to Barry's next of kin, his brother Hubert. Should he write to Hubert and inform him of the provisions of his Uncle George's will? In the end he decided to wait. There was always the possibility that Hubert might approach him first.

On the following Sunday Seabird was as usual in port. At lunch-time Docking went to the Penwarnes' house and, as he had expected, found all four brothers at home. After a few words with them, he asked Mark to come and see him when he had finished his meal.

Mark duly arrived at the constable's house, and Docking took him into his office. "What do you want to see me about, Mr. Docking?" Mark asked.

"I've got something to tell you," Docking replied. "And it's not very good news, I'm afraid. Barry Benson was killed on Thursday evening."

"I'm more than sorry to hear that," said Mark. "Barry and I always got on very well. What was it? A road accident?"

"No, it wasn't that," Docking replied. "He was stabbed to death in a pub."

Mark frowned. "Barry was always too fond of going into pubs. I never go into them myself because, like my three brothers, I'm a teetotaller. Did Barry get mixed up in a scrap?"

"Hardly that, from what I've been told," Docking replied. "He was trying to disarm a man who was brandishing a bottle, and the man stuck a knife into him."

"It was plucky of Barry to tackle the chap," said Mark. "Have the police got him?"

"Not yet, I gather," Docking replied. "But I expect they will before long. When are you going out again?"

"To-morrow morning's tide," said Mark. "We're going to fish about a hundred miles to the westward of the Scillies, which is farther than we usually go. Jake says that we shan't be in again until Thursday evening's tide. And now I must be getting along. Thank you for telling me about Barry, Mr. Docking."

Monday morning's tide was a few minutes before eight o'clock. Docking was patrolling the quay by six. He had devised a pretext for being about at that hour. He stopped at each craft he came to, and called out. "There's a dog reported missing. A white wire-haired terrier. He hasn't got aboard you, by any chance?"

Naturally no one had seen the fictitious dog, and the replies were in the negative. Docking reached Seabird, and repeated the question. Jake answered him. "No, we haven't got your dog. There's nobody but the four of us on board."

One by one, as they floated, the craft cast off from the quay and put out to sea. Seabird, drawing more water than most of them, was one of the last to leave. There was practically no wind, and she had to depend upon her engine. Noisily she passed out of the harbour.

On the following Thursday evening the tide was at five minutes past eleven. Docking was on the quay by nine o'clock. The sun was setting after a fine day with a pleasant breeze. He had not been there very long when he saw a sail out to sea, approaching the harbour. As the craft came closer, he recognised Seabird. The sail was lowered, and with the engine started, Seabird came alongside. After a while four men came ashore. Docking satisfied himself that they were the Penwarnes.

So things went on. Seabird came and went on her lawful occasions, carrying no one but the Penwarnes. Until the evening of 23rd August. Seabird had sailed on the previous Monday morning, with the four Penwarnes on board. The evening tide on the 23rd was just before midnight, and Seabird, her light burning brightly, came in at a quarter to eleven.

It was a dark evening, slightly hazy and with no moon. Docking, who had been on the lookout, concealed himself in the doorway of one of the houses facing the quay. After a while three men came ashore. Docking recognised them as Jake, Amos and Mark Penwarne. Where was Lew? Possibly he had been left on board to keep watch, though such a thing had never happened before.

Docking stayed where he was. The evening grew darker, and he had no fear of being seen in his place of concealment. It was not until the church clock struck twelve that his patience was rewarded. A shadowy figure appeared on Seabird's deck, then stepped ashore, and started to walk along the quay.

There was just sufficient light for Docking to see that, although the man was dressed as a fisherman, he was not Lew Penwarne. He was carrying a suitcase which from the way it weighed him down, seemed to be distinctly on the heavy side. He walked along the quay until he reached the head of the harbour. Docking, keeping as close as possible to the houses, followed him at a respectful distance.

At the head of the harbour the man turned to the left and, at the edge of the village, took the road which led to Cliff Cottage. Was the cottage his destination? Docking wondered. If so, it seemed that he must be unaware of George Hawken's death. What would he do when he found the cottage locked and unoccupied?

The man stopped, put down his suitcase, and stretched himself. Then after a minute or two, he picked up the suitcase and started laboriously up the slope. His actions were sufficient proof that he had no idea that he was being watched. For a quarter of a mile or so the road was open, affording no means of concealment. Fearing that the man might look back and perceive that he was followed, Docking did not move until the man was swallowed up in the darkness. Then he continued his pursuit.

At length he reached the dilapidated farm buildings which Arnold had noticed. The front of these stood right on the road. Suddenly, to Docking's amazement, a light appeared among the ruins. Could the man have turned in there and switched on a torch? Docking went on for a few yards, then concealed himself round the corner of the buildings. He could no longer see the light, but he could hear sounds .These culminated in a metallic clang, not unlike the noise of a dustbin lid, but deeper. Docking peeped round the corner of his hiding-place. In a minute or two the man reappeared on the road. He set off by the way he had come, swinging his suitcase lightly in his hand. Docking followed, gradually closing upon his quarry as he entered the village. The man turned along the quay, boarded Seabird, and disappeared down below.

Docking went back to his house, in two minds what he should do. The super wouldn't thank him for disturbing him at such a time of night. On the other hand, his orders were that he was to be informed immediately if anything was heard of Battlesby. Docking decided to risk it. He rang up, not Thramsbury Police Station, but Egford's private number. A minute or two elapsed before he heard a sleepy and irritable voice, which he recognised as the superintendent's. "Who's that and what do you want?"

"Constable Docking, speaking from Port Bosun, sir," Docking replied. "A man whom I'm pretty sure must have been Battlesby, came ashore from Seabird this evening."

"The devil he did!" Egford exclaimed. "Where is he now?"

"On board Seabird, sir," Docking replied. "But I have every reason to believe that while he was on shore he left something behind him."

"Confound the fellow," said Egford. "Why couldn't he have played his pranks at a more reasonable hour? All right, I'll come along. Wait for me in the village."

He rang off. Docking left his house and took up a position at the head of the harbour. The superintendent would have to pass that way, as would Battlesby if he came ashore again. The night was very still, and there was nobody about. No sound came from the craft tied up alongside the quay.

In rather less than half an hour Docking saw the headlights of a car approaching him from the direction of Thramsbury. Docking went out to the middle of the road, where the lights must fall upon him. The car reached him and pulled up. Egford put his head out of the window.

"Well, Constable, what's all this about?" he asked. "You haven't dragged me out of bed on a wild-goose chase, have you?"

"I hope not, sir," Docking replied. "I wouldn't have disturbed you if I hadn't been sure that the man I saw must have been Battlesby."

"Get in beside me and make your report," said Egford.

Docking did so, and described what he had seen and heard. "The suitcase was heavy when he went to the ruins, sir, and light when he came back. I don't think that there's any doubt that he left something there."

"We'll go and look," said Egford. "Show me where these ruins are."

Docking directed him up the road, and they pulled up outside the derelict farmhouse, where they alighted. Both had their torches, and with their aid they made their way into the ruins, to be confronted by a shapeless mass of broken down brickwork and rafters. Egford looked round.

"There's no metal here," he said. "Are you quite sure that it was a metallic clang you heard?"

"Quite sure, sir," Docking replied. "There's a yard at the back. There may be some sheets of corrugated iron lying there."

The back wall of the ruin had completely collapsed. The two men climbed over the debris to find themselves in a space which had once been enclosed by a wall. Swinging their torches round, they could see no loose sheets of corrugated iron or indeed any other loose metal. But the light of Egford's torch showed him, at one end of the yard, an iron manhole-cover level with the ground. He pointed this out to Docking. "What's that for, do you suppose?" he asked.

"I expect it's the cover of the old cesspit, sir," Docking replied. "There was no main drainage here when these premises were occupied."

"See if you can lift it," said Egford. "And, if you can, drop it again when you have raised it a few inches."

Docking applied himself to the cover. It was not, as might have been expected, rusted to its seating, and he had no difficulty in raising it. Having done so, he let it fall again. It dropped to its original position with a loud clang. "Is that like the sound you heard?" Egford asked.

"Exactly, sir," Docking replied. "In fact, that was it, I'm sure."

"Then lift the cover clear and lay it aside," said Egford. "Then we shall see what's under it."

Docking removed the cover, and he and Egford directed their torches into the aperture. The pit had been filled up with rubble to within a couple of feet of the ground level. On the surface of the rubble lay a rectangular object, the nature of which it was difficult to determine.

"Whatever that is, see if you can lift it out," said Egford.

Docking knelt down beside the pit and plunged his arms into it. The object was heavy and awkward to handle, but he lifted it out and deposited it on the ground. It turned out to be a flat metal box, secured by a padlock.

"Just about the size and shape to fit into the suitcase the man was carrying, sir," Docking remarked.

"Why did he leave it here?" Egford asked. "Presumably because he meant to recover it later on. Not a bad hiding-place meanwhile. But why did he want to hide it? We shall have to find out what's inside."

"I expect the man's got the key of the padlock in his pocket, sir," Docking replied.

"I expect he has," Egford agreed. "But I don't propose to ask him for it. We could file through the hasp of the padlock. That is, if we had a file."

"I've got one at home that would do the trick, sir," said Docking.

"Very well, then," Egford replied. "We'll take the box to your house and open it there. I'll give you a hand to carry it to the car."

The box was awkward to carry, since it had no handle. But between them they got it to the car. Having placed it in the back, they drove to the constable's house, where they deposited the box on the office table. Docking went out and returned with a triangular file, with which he attacked the hasp of the padlock. He very soon filed it through, and was able to open the lid of the box. This revealed a sheet of rubber, exactly fitting the box. "Lift that out and let's see what's underneath," said Egford.

Docking lifted out the rubber. Beneath it the box was tightly packed with small objects, each wrapped in tissue paper. Egford picked out one of these and unwrapped it, to find a Swiss wrist-watch. "So that's it!" he exclaimed. "The man is a smuggler. I wonder the Customs haven't caught him out before now."

"The Customs don't search the fishing-boats, sir," Docking replied. "They don't have any need to. The boats don't put in to any foreign port. They just go out fishing and come back here to land their catches."

"The man knew that, of course," said Egford. "That's why he fixed up his dodge for bringing the stuff over. Well, we'd better look through this little lot before we go any further."

They took out the objects one by one and unwrapped them. They all turned out to be Swiss watches of one kind or another.

"Not a bad haul," said Egford. "I suppose, strictly speaking, we ought to turn the matter over to the Customs, but we'll keep it to ourselves for the present. Put the things back in the box."

When this was done, they put the box in the boot of the car. "Jump in," said Egford. "You've got a pair of handcuffs in your pocket? Very well, then. We'll go and interview the owner of the box."

They drove on to the quay, and pulled up at the spot where Seabird was tied up. There they alighted and went on board. The companion-door was open, and they went below. By the light of their torches they found in the saloon a man asleep in one of the bunks. Egford shook him roughly and the man woke up. With the torches shining on his face he could see nothing.

"Who are you, and what do you want?" he demanded.

"We want you," Egford replied. "What's your name?"

"Battlesby," the man replied. "I'm a friend of the Penwarnes. I've been out with them, helping them to fish."

"Where is Lew Penwarne?" Egford asked.

"How should I know?" Battlesby replied. "He wasn't on board on this voyage. He stayed on shore, I suppose."

"He didn't," said Egford. "He was on board when Seabird left port. I suggest to you that he is on board the French fishing-boat, Marie Touchet?"

"I don't know what you're talking about," Battlesby replied sulkily.

"You know very well," said Egford. "You sailed from Les Baleines in the Marie Touchet and transferred to Seabird at sea. Lew took your place in the French boat. What have you to say to that?"

Battlesby showed obvious signs of uneasiness, but made no reply. A large suitcase was standing beside the bunk. Egford pointed to this. "This is your property, I take it?" he said. "What is in it?"

"What do you suppose?" Battlesby replied. "My shore-going kit, of course."

"Get up and put on your shore-going kit," said Egford.

Very reluctantly Battlesby climbed out of his bunk. Hanging from a deck beam in the centre of the saloon was an oil-lamp. Docking took a box of matches from his pocket and lighted it.

"That's better," said Egford. "Now we can see what we're doing. Now will you kindly open your suitcase, Mr. Battlesby."

"I don't see why I should," Battlesby replied. "I'm not going ashore."

"I'm not so sure of that," said Egford. "Open the suitcase, anyhow."

Battlesby lifted the lid of the suitcase, revealing the fact that it was completely empty. "I remember now!" he exclaimed. "I took my kit out of the case and stowed it in the locker."

"Well, get it out," said Egford.

Battlesby opened the locker under the bunk. There was nothing in it but an oilskin and a sou'-wester. "Well, that's queer," he muttered. "The Penwarnes must have taken my kit ashore by mistake."

"Careless of them," said Egford. "Never mind. Put on your sea-going kit instead."

A pair of trousers and a jersey lay at the foot of the bunk. With a very ill grace Battlesby put these on. "Now what do you want?" he asked.

"You're going ashore with us," said Egford.

"I shall do nothing of the kind," Battlesby replied defiantly. "Why should I?"

"Because I say so," said Egford. "Now, don't let's have any

nonsense. There are two of us, and we shall carry you ashore if you attempt any resistance." Docking took the handcuffs from his pocket and dangled them before Battlesby's eyes.

"This is an outrage, and you will suffer for it," he exclaimed. "You are interfering in affairs of state. I am a secret service agent, employed by the Government. You coerce me at your own risk."

"I'll chance that," said Egford. "Now come along quietly, and don't compel us to use force."

Battlesby allowed himself to be led up on deck, and thence on to the quay.

"Get into the back of the car with him, Constable," said Egford. "And if he tries to play any tricks, clap the bracelets on to him. We're going to take you for a drive, Mr. Battlesby."

Docking hustled Battlesby into the back of the car, while Egford climbed into the driving seat. They set off and reached Thramsbury Police Station. Battlesby remained sullenly silent during the journey. He was taken to Egford's room, where a constable mounted guard over him. Docking took the box from the boot of the car, and as he laid it on the table Battlesby's expression showed signs of horrified amazement.

"Now then, Mr. Battlesby," said Egford. "This box and its contents are your property, I believe?"

Battlesby did his best to recover his composure. "I don't know what you're talking about," he replied. "I've never seen that box before."

"That is not the truth," said Egford sternly. "You imagine that your movements about midnight were not seen but in fact they were. You came ashore from Seabird, carrying your suitcase, in which was this box. You went to the ruined farm buildings on the road leading to Cliff Cottage and entered them. There you opened the suitcase and took from it the box, which you deposited in the disused cesspit in the yard. Then carrying the empty suitcase you returned to Seabird, without the slightest apprehension. That is the truth."

Battlesby looked utterly dumbfounded. It was quite obvious that this revelation was utterly unexpected. But he did not abandon the struggle. "It's all a most ghastly mistake," he muttered.

"Trying to evade the Customs is always a mistake," said

Egford quietly. "That box contains a quantity of Swiss watches, which you brought over from the Continent. You will be detained in custody, pending further investigations. Take him away, Constable."

The constable marched Battlesby from the room, and Egford turned to Docking.

"You'd better stay here for what remains of the night," he said. "You can doss down in one of the cells, if you like. You shall be driven back to Port Bosun in the morning. Don't tell the Penwarnes what has become of their passenger. Let them think that he has disappeared of his own accord."

At nine o'clock on Thursday morning Egford rang up Scotland Yard and asked to speak to Arnold. He was put through to Arnold's room.

"Good morning, Mr. Arnold," he said. "I've some news for you. We've got Battlesby, who turns out to be not a secret service agent, but a smuggler. He's safely under lock and key. You'll like to see him, I expect?"

"Very much indeed," Arnold replied. "I'll be with you this evening."

Chapter XVII

As soon as Egford had rung off, Arnold put a call through to High Eldersham Hall. A familiar voice answered him. "This is Merrion speaking. Who are you?"

"Arnold speaking from the Yard," Arnold replied. "Battlesby has turned up and is at Thramsbury. Does your offer still hold good?"

"Rather!" Merrion exclaimed. "I'll start off in the car in ten minutes' time, and call for you at the Yard. Then we'll go on to Thramsbury. We should get there in the late afternoon."

He was as good as his word. He called for Arnold before noon, and they went on their way without delay. Merrion was a fast, though careful driver, and they reached Thramsbury by five o'clock, They stopped at the police station, where they found Egford.

"Well, here I am," said Arnold. "Let me introduce my friend Desmond Merrion, who drove me down. He has given me the greatest help with the Hawken case. You won't mind if he is present at our conversations?"

"Not in the least," Egford replied. "I am very pleased to meet you, Mr. Merrion. Excuse me a moment."

He picked up his telephone and rang through to Docking, who had returned to Port Bosun that morning.

"Is that you, Constable? I'm sending the car to fetch you. You are to come here at once. What time is Seabird due to sail?"

"On to-night's tide, sir," Docking replied. "And that won't be before ten o'clock."

"Then you can bring one of the Penwarnes with you," said Egford. "Mark preferably, since he and I have met before. You can promise him that we'll return him to Port Bosun before Seabird is due to sail."

He rang off, and gave Arnold a brief account of the previous night's events.

"Battlesby won't own up to anything," he went on. "But there's no doubt that he was engaged in smuggling. He was searched after he was brought here, and a small key was found in one of his trouser-pockets. That key fits the padlock with which the box was secured. Leaving no doubt that the box and its contents are his."

"But what was his object in hiding the box in the ruins?" Arnold asked.

"To keep it in safety until he was ready to retrieve it," Egford replied. "No doubt he intended to return to the Continent by transferring from Seabird to the Marie Touchet. Later he would have returned to this country by some orthodox route, and probably under a different name. He would then have gone to Port Bosun, probably by car, picked up the box, and taken it to wherever he expected to be able to sell the stuff. London, most likely."

They were still discussing the possibilities when Docking arrived, bringing Mark Penwarne with him.

"Sit down, Penwarne," said Egford. "We want to ask you a question or two. You brought Mr. Battlesby with you when you came in from your last voyage, didn't you?"

"That's right," Mark replied. "We met the Marie Touchet at the usual place. Mr. Battlesby boarded us from her, and Lew took his place. We shall meet her again to-morrow. Mr. Battlesby will go aboard her, and we shall take off Lew. I haven't seen Mr. Battlesby all day, but I don't doubt he'll come aboard Seabird before sailing time."

"He won't do that," said Egford. "I recommend you not to wait for him. Did he ever open his suitcase while he was on board Seabird?"

Mark shook his head. "That I couldn't say. I don't recollect ever having seen him open it."

"So you don't know what was in it?" Egford asked.

"Mr. Battlesby told us on the first trip he went with us, that he carried important and secret documents in it," Mark replied. "Naturally, he didn't show them to us."

"Well, we needn't keep you any longer," said Egford. "You'll be glad to get back, I dare say. The car which brought you here is waiting to take you back to Port Bosun. Take Penwarne out, Constable, and then come back here."

Docking led Mark from the room, and Egford turned to Arnold.

"It's a perfectly clear case. I shall bring Battlesby before the

Bench to-morrow, charged with bringing Swiss watches into the country without paying duty on them. I shall ask for a remand for a few days, as we shall want the Penwarnes to give evidence. But you're wanting to see the man, Mr. Arnold. I'll send for him."

He pressed a button on his desk, and a sergeant appeared. "Bring in Mr. Battlesby, Sergeant," said Egford.

The sergeant went out, to return in a few minutes with Battlesby. He seemed to be unsubdued by his confinement, and looked round the room defiantly. But when his eyes fell upon Arnold, he stiffened, and a hunted look came into his eyes. As for Arnold, he stared at him incredulously. Could it be, or was it merely a striking resemblance? No, there was no doubt about it.

"Good afternoon, Mr. Benson," said Arnold. "I did not expect to meet you here."

"My name is Battlesby, not Benson," the other replied in a voice which had risen to a high falsetto.

"Oh, come now," said Arnold reprovingly. "You and I know each other well enough. Why not admit that your name is Hubert Benson?"

This elicited no reply. Merrion's smile expressed his satisfaction. His imagination had not led him astray. "May I be allowed to talk to Mr. Benson?" he asked.

Arnold and Egford glanced at each other. "I have no objection," Arnold replied. "What about you, Mr. Egford?"

The revelation of his true identity had obviously been a bitter blow to Hubert. Sweat was trickling down his face, and he was swaying on his feet, as though about to fall.

"Give Mr. Benson a chair, Constable," said Egford. "I have no objection to Mr. Merrion talking to him."

Hubert was provided with a chair, into which he sank limply.

"Where were you when your Uncle George was killed, Mr. Benson?" Merrion asked.

"I was in France, in the course of my business," Hubert replied. "I am an import and export merchant and I have to maintain contact with the customers to whom I sell goods and with the firms from whom I buy them."

"Exactly," said Merrion. "But it would appear that the import side of your business is not always legal. Let us go back to 14th June, the date on which your uncle was killed. Previous to that date you had been in France. But you had returned to England by transferring from the Marie Touchet to Seabird.

"You had brought with you a consignment of goods, contained in your suitcase, and you had no intention of paying duty upon them. You landed at Port Bosun soon after eight on the morning of 14th June, taking your suitcase with you. From the quay you walked along the road leading to Cliff Cottage until you came to the ruined farmhouse. You deposited your suitcase in the disused cesspit in the yard there, then came out and continued on your way towards Cliff Cottage.

"While you were still some little distance away, you saw your uncle come out of the cottage, carrying his shooting-stick and sketching block. It was evident to you that he was going sketching. Your uncle may not have noticed you or, if he did, he did not recognise you in the fisherman's clothes you were wearing. Your uncle took the path leading to the ledge in the face of the cliff. You allowed your uncle to pass out of your sight, then followed him.

"You had intended to murder your uncle in Cliff Cottage, and for that purpose you had brought a length of cord with you, probably a lanyard taken from Seabird. But you appreciated that the fact that he had gone out would make it possible for you to make his death appear accidental. You followed the ledge until, on rounding a boulder, you came upon your uncle. He was sitting on his shooting-stick, with his back turned to you.

"In your rubber boots you moved silently. You crept up behind your uncle, slipped the loop of the cord over his head, and pulled tightly on the ends of it. The stricture of the cord round him caused your victim to lose consciousness, and he fell from his stick on to the ground. You removed the cord and put it in your pocket. Your uncle was no longer capable of resistance, and you rolled him over the cliff."

Merrion's manner was suave and quiet, far more damaging than any form of bluster. As he spoke, Hubert's cheeks lost every vestige of colour. He opened his lips to reply, but Egford interposed quickly "It is my duty to warn you that anything you say may be used in evidence."

Hubert paid no heed to this warning. "You can't prove a word of what you've said!" he exclaimed, again in that queer shrill voice. "Why should I have wished to murder my uncle?"

"You had a most powerful motive," said Merrion. "I am inclined to believe that your business was not prospering and that you were in financial straits. The visit of your wife to Moat Barn suggests that she was aware of this, and was endeavouring to enlist your Uncle Matthew's aid on your behalf. But to return to your doings on that day. You returned to the ruins, took your smuggled goods from the suitcase, and concealed them in the cesspit. The empty suitcase you took away with you. Later in the day you returned to Seabird, and sailed in her on the evening tide. In due course you transferred to the Marie Touchet, and disembarked from her at Les Baleines. From there you made your way by stages to Paris.

"There you received the letter from your secretary informing you of your Uncle George's death. You simulated a great concern. Your obvious duty was to break the news to your Uncle Matthew. You flew to England and drove to Moat Barn. You knew that Sir Matthew had left a considerable part of his estate to his brother. Now that his brother was dead, his existing will had become ineffective. You believed that if he should die before he had time to make another, you and your brother would become joint heirs to his estate.

"You had already determined that Sir Matthew should die. Not immediately following your visit to Moat Barn, because that might have seemed suspicious, but within the next few days. While in France you had procured some potassium cyanide, and this you had made up into a tablet resembling those which Sir Matthew took regularly. In the course of your visit to Moat Barn, you found an opportunity of inspecting the box of tablets which stood on Sir Matthew's bedside table. You saw that it was full, or nearly so. You inserted your tablet into the box, not on the top, but under the harmless tablets which it contained. You knew that sooner or later Miss Paris, as you believed her to be, would pick out your tablet and give it to Sir Matthew.

"Things fell out as you had planned. By 12th July your tablet had become uncovered and lay nearest to Miss Paris's hand. Unsuspectingly, she picked it out and gave it to Sir Matthew, to whom it proved fatal. No suspicion fell upon you, because you could prove that you were in London at the time of Sir Matthew's death.

"Soon after your interview with Sir Matthew, you drove to Port Bosun, arriving there in the hours of darkness, and having your empty suitcase in the car. You entered the ruined farmhouse, and transferred the goods you had concealed in the cesspit to the suitcase. You then drove back to London where, no doubt, you disposed of the goods at a considerable profit.

"After Sir Matthew's death you felt secure. You learnt that he had destroyed his first will and had not made another. You believed that he had died an intestate bachelor, and that you and your brother would share his estate. Barry had disappeared, and you may have believed that he would never turn up to claim his inheritance. But, inconveniently for you, Barry did turn up, and would certainly claim his share. I think it was when he called on you that the idea came to you. If Barry were to die, you would be left in sole enjoyment of Sir Matthew's estate.

"You professed the utmost friendship for him, advanced him money, and asked him to tell you where he was lodging. He did tell you, and from that time you watched the neighbourhood. You saw Barry going to the Ninepins on two evenings in succession, and on the third evening you took action. You had probably explored the premises in the daytime, and saw that the bar was divided in two, one part for coloured men, and the other for white.

"You made yourself a simple but effective mask and bought a pair of rubber gloves. On the evening in question you put on a raincoat and the gloves, carrying the mask in your pocket. Under the raincoat you had hidden a knife, which you had recently sharpened. Thus attired, you were in no way conspicuous, and you mingled with the crowd in Borough High Street. You saw your brother come along, and turn into the street in which the Ninepins is situated.

"You waited until very few people were passing up and down that street, then went towards the Ninepins. Just before you got there, you slipped the mask over your face. Then you burst open the door and rushed in, shouting, 'Down with the colour bar!' It is noticeable that in moments of excitement, your voice rises to a high pitch.

"A bottle stood on the counter. You picked this up and aimed a blow at the landlord, who dodged aside. Then you turned on three men who were standing by the counter and felled one of them with the bottle. The other two escaped. At this point your brother came towards you, obviously with the intention of depriving you of the bottle. You drew the knife from beneath your raincoat and with it stabbed your brother to the heart. You then ran out of the Ninepins, tore off your mask and threw it away."

Arnold and Egford had listened in amazement. Merrion's accusation had been so confident that it seemed that he must have been an eye-witness of the events which he had described. After he had come to an end, a few seconds of silence ensued. Then Egford spoke.

"Remember that you have been cautioned, Mr. Benson. Have you anything to reply to what you have just heard?"

But Hubert was in no condition to say anything. He had slumped forward in his chair to such an extent that his face was invisible, and he was shuddering violently. He seemed not to hear the question which Egford had put to him.

"Take him away, Sergeant," said Egford.

The sergeant lifted Hubert from his chair. He staggered on his feet, and would have fallen had not the sergeant held him up by both arms. Egford rose.

"I'll lend you a hand, Sergeant," he said. Between them they almost carried Hubert from the room and deposited him on the cot in his cell.

Egford came back to the room. "He's barely half-conscious," he said. "You knocked him clean out, Mr. Merrion. But I can't understand how you knew."

"I didn't know," Merrion replied. "But I felt on fairly safe ground in saying what I did."

"What put you on to it?" Arnold asked.

Merrion smiled. "My imagination, as usual. It had struck me as significant that the so-called Battlesby came from France and returned there at a time when Hubert Benson was known to be on the Continent. Battlesby had the opportunity of murdering George Hawken, but his motive was far from clear. When you recognised Battlesby as Benson, I knew that my guess had been right. The motive was sufficiently explained.

"As you know, I have always maintained that both Hawken brothers were murdered by the same person. But how could

Benson have murdered Sir Matthew? His alibi at the time of Sir Matthew's death was unimpeachable. I considered this for a long time before a possibility dawned upon me.

"From the first it had seemed probable that Sir Matthew's death had been due to swallowing a poisonous tablet taken from the box in which his digestive tablets were contained. At last I saw that it not necessarily followed that that tablet had been put in the box on the day of Sir Matthew's death. If it had been inserted beneath a number of the harmless tablets, there would have been some delay. Lady Hawken would have picked out each tablet as it came. It would have been some days before she got down to the fatal one. Benson had been at Moat Barn some days before Sir Matthew's death.

"I'm bound to confess that I didn't at once tumble to the idea that Benson had murdered his brother. He had a motive for so doing. He believed that Barry's death would double his own inheritance. It was not until I heard that queer high note in his voice that I realised the truth."

"There is no doubt that he's guilty," said Egford. "The way he collapsed is sufficient proof of that. What do you suggest that we do with him, Mr. Arnold?"

"Let him stew in his own juice until the morning," Arnold replied. "If he turns obstinate, you can bring him before the Bench on a charge of evading the Customs, and ask for a remand in custody."

"I don't think that there's much obstinacy left in him," said Egford. "You'll stay here overnight? You can put up at the Three Lions."

"I'll do that," Arnold replied. "What about you, Merrion?"

"I'll stay with you," said Merrion. "Then, when your business has come to a satisfactory end, I can drive you back to London."

Next morning after breakfast Arnold and Merrion returned to the police station, where they found Egford.

"I hope you both had a good night," said Egford. "Since I had been up nearly all of the previous night, I slept like a log. If you're ready, I'll send for Benson."

Arnold expressed his readiness, and Egford pressed the button on his desk. The sergeant appeared and was told to bring in the prisoner. In a few minutes he came back, leading Hubert by the arm. He had changed so much in appearance that Arnold could hardly believe that this was the man he had interviewed at Rutland House. His arrogant manner had left him, and his face had become haggard and drawn. He looked so weak and trembling that it would have been inhuman not to allow him to sit down.

"Give him a chair, Sergeant," said Egford.

The sergeant brought forward a chair, and Hubert sank limply into it. "Now, Mr. Benson," said Egford, "Would you care to make a statement?"

Hubert shook his head. "What's the use?" he asked despairingly. "Everything that was said yesterday was true. I can put up no defence."

"You confess to having murdered first Mr. George Hawken, then Sir Matthew Hawken, and finally your brother Barry Benson?" Egford asked.

"What can I do but confess?" Hubert replied. "You seem to know everything, though how you found out passes my comprehension."

"Will you write out a brief account of the facts and sign it?" Egford asked.

"I am ready to do that," Hubert replied. "I don't very much care what the consequences will be. My business has for some time been in such a serious state that I am now on the verge of bankruptcy. And the fact that I committed three murders under the false impression that they would save me is not a pleasant one to contemplate."

That morning Hubert was brought before the Bench, charged with the evasion of paying duty. Egford and Docking gave evidence, and the box of watches was produced. Egford asked for a remand in custody, which was granted, on Egford explaining that further and more serious charges would be made.

Early in the following week Hubert appeared once more in court. He had written out a statement, which Egford produced. Asked if he had anything to say at that stage, Hubert shook his head and said, "Nothing!" He was committed for trial at the next assizes. At his trial his demeanour was one of complete indifference. Evidence was given of his arrival at Port Bosun, of his visit to Moat Barn, and of the scene in the Ninepins. Hubert's counsel submitted that there was no case against his client, since there had been no witnesses of any one of the three alleged murders. The judge overruled this, and instructed the jury to be guided by the prisoner's statement. The jury, after a very short deliberation, returned a verdict of guilty. The death sentence was passed, and Hubert was duly executed.

Merrion received news of Shepherd Green from Luke Dedham, with whom he regularly corresponded. "Mavis will be amused by what I have to tell you," Luke wrote in a letter received by Merrion shortly after the execution. "Since Amabel Aintree learnt that Francine is Lady Hawken, her attitude towards her has been completely reversed. Francine is no longer a disreputable hussy, but a lady of title, worthy of every consideration. Amabel has become a frequent visitor to Moat Barn, and she does not always go there by herself.

"Her half-brother, Dick Leiston, much younger than herself, has recently come back from a long residence in the Far East. Dick is unassuming, good looking and a keen cricketer. He has already proved an invaluable member of our club. And, while on the subject of cricket, I am expecting you and Mavis to come and stay with me for our week next year. And let us profoundly hope that it will not be marred by tragedy, as it was this year.

"But I am digressing. To return to Dick. The firm by whom he is employed have appointed him to a post in London. He is living at the manor, and goes up to London five days a week. During the week-ends he frequently accompanies Amabel to Moat Barn, and, from what I have heard, and seen, he and Francine get on very well together."

Merrion continued to receive at intervals letters from Luke. Shortly before Christmas one came, written obviously in a mood of satisfaction.

"What I have been expecting for some time has come to pass. Francine has just been here to see me. She told me that she had the most wonderful news for me. Dick had asked her to marry him, and she had agreed. I asked her if she was sure that she would be happy with Dick, and she replied that she knew she would be. She was in love with Dick, and she was certain that he was in love with her. Besides, though that consideration had not weighed with her, she was becoming desperately lonely at Moat Barn all by herself. She had insisted that the wedding should not take place until at least a year after Sir Matthew's death.

"When they are married, she and Dick are to live at Moat Barn. Francine told me that she would hate to leave the place. Meanwhile, an architect is to prepare plans for converting that vast studio into reception rooms, with bedrooms above. Amabel has asked her to stay at the manor while the work is being carried out.

"Green, the art dealer has been to see Francine more than once. He has persuaded her to sell him the pictures which Sir Matthew had collected, including the Sisley which Arnold rescued from his clutches. But Francine has refused to sell any of Sir Matthew's own pictures. She says that even after the alterations, there will be plenty of room to hang them.

"The domestic staff will remain as before. Francine tells me that nothing would induce her to part with either Albert Oakley or Mrs. Toogood. I don't think she knows that it was Mrs. Toogood who revealed her secret to Arnold. If she does, she bears no resentment. She has even persuaded that old tippler, Charlie Potter, to resume his work in the garden.

"The wedding will probably take place immediately after our cricket week. Since you and Mavis have already accepted my invitation you will meet the happy couple. I am sure that you will like them as well as I do."

CPSIA information can be obtained at www.ICGtesting.com
Printed in the USA
LVOW13s1726171013

357412LV00007B/1129/P